CARA COLTER
The Playboy's Plain Jane

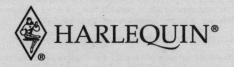

TORONTO • NEW YORK • LONDON
AMSTERDAM • PARIS • SYDNEY • HAMBURG
STOCKHOLM • ATHENS • TOKYO • MILAN • MADRID
PRAGUE • WARSAW • BUDAPEST • AUCKLAND

ISBN-13: 978-0-373-17495-9
ISBN-10:   0-373-17495-0

THE PLAYBOY'S PLAIN JANE

First North American Publication 2008.

www.eHarlequin.com

Printed in U.S.A.

**A few words from Cara about writing
this book:**

"I love flowers. To me, one of the most luxurious
feelings in the world is to have a lovely, fresh
bouquet on the dining room table. I even have
a special light fixture that I can turn on just to
spotlight the arrangement. The house might be a
mess, a deadline fast looming, but when I see those
flowers, breathe in their scent, for a moment my
soul goes still and I feel my world as sacred."

Cara Colter and her real-life hero, Rob, live on
an acreage in British Columbia. Their cat, Hunter,
graciously shares his house with them. They own
seven horses, including two new "babies"—Weiner
and Schnitzel, a pair of Fjord-cross colts. Visit
Cara (and the horses, cat and Rob) at her Web site,
www.Cara-Colter.com.

**Cara's next book will whisk you away
to a stunningly exotic royal island!**
Her Royal Wedding Wish—June 08
Only from Harlequin Romance®.

To my daughter-in-law, Crissy Martin,
A true original,
Funny, sensitive, spunky, beautiful

CHAPTER ONE

"…AND I THINK a few lilies," Mrs. Johnson said sadly, "Gertrude did love lilies."

Katie's eyes slid to the clock. Nearly one o'clock. She couldn't very well stop midorder—especially for something as sensitive as a funeral wreath—to go look out the window. But when Mrs. Johnson had come in a full ten minutes ago, she had indicated she was in a hurry. They should have been done by now!

Aware of a certain despicable powerlessness, Katie set down her pen. Well, she did own The Flower Girl, after all. She was the boss. If she wanted to go look out the window, she could do that!

"Excuse me for just a sec," she said. "Something in the window, um, needs my immediate attention."

Ignoring Mrs. Johnson's bewildered glance toward a window that held an eye-catching display of nonattention-needing spring bouquets, Katie stepped out from behind the counter, walked swiftly to the window. She toyed with a vase of bright phlox that represented the new hopes and sweet dreams of the coming of spring.

Right on time, the man she despised more than any

other rounded the corner of First Street, onto Davis. Dylan McKinnon was coming fast, a man who would have scorned the word *jogging.* He was running flat-out, arms and legs pumping, his dark hair wind ruffled.

She felt the bottom fall out of her stomach. Today he was wearing a hooded black jacket, with no sleeves, the absolutely perfect outfit for a man with muscles like that. His arms rippled with easy strength, the line of his triceps, hard cut and sweat beaded, did a funny thing to Katie's breathing.

The jacket was designed to show off his attributes, obviously. As were the shorts, showing the perfect line of legs that were strong and hard with lean male muscle.

Pathetic, she chided herself, knowing darn well it was not Dylan McKinnon she despised, but her own weakness.

He was trouble with a million-dollar grin, but it just didn't make him any less bewitching.

His hair, the rich dark color of espresso, was a touch too long. It made her think ridiculous thoughts of the long-ago Scottish warriors who, with a name like McKinnon, had been Dylan's ancestors.

He had a strong nose, and a faintly clefted chin, high cheekbones that were whisker roughened today. And stamped across those perfect, breath-stealing features was an expression of fierce determination, an almost frightening singleness of focus.

His eyes, framed with a sinful abundance of black, soot-dipped lash, and bluer than the sky right before the sun faded from it, had that look of a man who was looking inward to his own strength, as well as outward at his world.

Katie hated how she loved to watch him run, but

Dylan McKinnon wasn't the most eligible bachelor in Hillsboro, Ontario, for no reason.

Don't stop, she silently begged as he slowed near her window. She pulled back so that he wouldn't see she had watched, darted for the counter as she read his intention to come into her store. He opened the door just as she managed to get behind the cash register and slam her glasses back on her face.

She peeked up over the rims of her spectacles at him, trying to hide the raggedness of her breathing from her unscheduled sprint behind the counter.

"I'm just taking an order," she said, no-nonsense, *professional.* "I'll be with you shortly."

The grin erased some of the warrior from his face, but the lifted eyebrow reinforced it, said as clearly as though he had spoken, *No mere woman has ever kept the great McKinnon waiting.*

She pursed her lips to let him know others might be bowled over by his charms, but she was not. She did feel weakly compelled to watch his daily run, which he surely never had to know. He had to wait in line like everyone else.

Mrs. Johnson, however, wrecked Katie's intention to humble him. Obvious recognition dawned in her face. "Oh, no," she said breathlessly, forgetting her hurry, "You go first, Mr. McKinnon."

"Dylan, please. Are you sure?" He smiled at Mrs. Johnson with chocolate-melting charm.

"Oh," she stammered. "Of course, I'm sure."

"Katie, my lady," he said, stepping up to the counter, with his all-male swagger.

She steeled herself against that smile. "Mr. McKinnon."

"What do you think of the new jacket?" he asked, just as if he hadn't jumped the line, just as if he wasn't taking another customer's time.

She glanced at it, saw close-up the way it showed every line of muscle in his arm, and gulped. As she dragged her eyes back up to his face, she saw the distinctive red Daredevils emblem on his chest. When she met his eyes, she was pretty sure he was conceited enough to know exactly what she thought of his new jacket. Now she wouldn't have given him the pleasure of telling him, even if there were goblins waiting in the back room to cut out her tongue if she uttered a lie.

"I would think, by definition, a jacket should have sleeves."

He frowned at her. "It's a running jacket. You want your arms free when you run. Plus, you don't want to overheat. Our engineers designed it. It's going into production next week."

"It has a hood," she pointed out.

"Uh, yeah?"

"So, your head might get cold, but your arms won't?"

He scowled at her. "Part of the reason it's designed without sleeves is the sweat issue."

"Sweat?" she echoed, hoping it didn't sound as if she was saying a dirty word.

"It's easier to clean an undershirt than the whole jacket." He unzipped, as if he was actually considering demonstrating, and it seemed as if her life had reached a new low. She was discussing undershirts with Dylan McKinnon.

She held up her hand before he managed to get the jacket off, and he lifted his eyebrows at her, faintly mocking, as if he had guessed she was too long without a man and given to swooning.

"Well," she said brightly, trying to hide her wild discomfort, "what can I do for you today?"

"Katie, my lady, I need you to just send a little something to, uh—"

"Heather," she said stiffly.

He grinned. "Yeah, Heather. Thanks."

"Message?" she asked.

"Uh—"

Katie rapidly calculated in her head. This was Heather's third bouquet. "Something like, Sorry I forgot?" she prompted him.

If he was the least contrite that his fickle heart was so predictable, he did not show it. He nodded, grinned at her with *approval.* "Perfect. Oh, and maybe send a little something to Tara, too."

Since his time with Heather was drawing to a close, she guessed cynically. Tara was always on the back burner. Poor Tara. Poor Heather.

He turned, gave Mrs. Johnson a friendly salute and went out the door. The flower shop, which had seemed cheerful and cozy only moments before, seemed faded and gray, hopelessly dreary, as if he had swept every bit of color and energy out of the room with him.

"Was that really Daredevil Dylan McKinnon of the Toronto Blue Jays?" Mrs. Johnson asked, wide-eyed.

Dylan McKinnon had not thrown a baseball in more than five years. In fact, in Katie's opinion, he had managed to parlay the shortest career in professional baseball in history into quite a bit more celebrity than he deserved.

"None other," she said reluctantly.

"My," Mrs. Johnson said. "My."

Young. Old. Whatever. Dylan McKinnon simply had that indefinable *thing* that made him irresistible to the opposite sex.

Pheromones, Katie told herself. He was emitting them with his sweat, a primitive, silent mating call that commanded a woman to choose the biggest, the strongest, the toughest. When he was that handsome, as well, the average woman had very little chance against him. For one with at least a modicum of brains, however, there was no excuse. Though there was no telling what would have happened if he had managed to get the jacket off!

Weakling, she berated herself silently. Outwardly she said "Now about Gertrude's wreath. What kind of lilies—"

"Does he live around here?" Mrs. Johnson asked eagerly. "My granddaughter is a great fan."

If you love your granddaughter, keep her away from that man. "I don't think he lives around here," Katie offered stiffly. In fact, the head office for his wildly successful sporting goods line was located behind a discreet bronze plaque that read McKinnon two doors down, but Katie saw no reason she should offer that. She'd never be able to find a parking spot if the location of the daredevil's office and empire became public knowledge to his rabid fans.

"Gertrude's flowers?" she prompted.

"Oh, yes."

"Since she liked lilies, what would you think of lily of the valley?" Katie asked. "They signify a return to happiness."

"Oh, my dear, that is so lovely. Thank you. One of the reasons I shop here is because you know these things."

In Victorian times, people had always associated meanings with flowers. Katie, as the flower girl, knew those meanings and loved working them into her arrangements.

"It will be a beautiful wreath," she promised. Already she could see the lilies woven together with babies' breath.

But she could also see Heather Richards's bouquet. Perhaps a few snapdragons scattered among yellow roses. A warning of deception and a decrease in love—not that a woman like Heather was ever going to get the meaning.

Like most of the women Dylan McKinnon showed interest in, if they hadn't had celebrity status before they showed up on his arm, they certainly did after. Heather, however, had held minor celebrity status before, as Miss Hillsboro Bikini. Katie would send some azaleas to Tara: *take care of yourself.*

"Dylan seemed to know you," Mrs. Johnson said, almost as if her mind had drifted right along with Katie's. And right back to him. "He did call you Katie, my lady."

"Mr. McKinnon is a very good customer."

"I think it's very sweet that he has a pet name for you."

"Well, Mr. McKinnon is a man who has being sweet to women down to a fine art." And she should know. She had been handling his flower orders since she had opened her shop two doors down from him, just over a year ago.

She didn't want to be mean-spirited about it, because Dylan McKinnon had always been nothing but charming to her. He had charm down to a science: when she was in the room with him it was hard not to give in to the heady sense that she was the only girl in his world, that he truly *cared* about her, that he genuinely found her interesting.

But, of course, that was precisely why he could get any woman he batted those amazing lashes at. Besides, he was one of her best customers, and he didn't just give her a great deal of business, but also spin-off business. Almost all his old girlfriends enjoyed the quality and imaginativeness of her flower arrangements so much that they became her customers.

But she was sure Mrs. Johnson wouldn't look quite so smitten—ready to deliver her granddaughter in gift wrap and a bow—if she knew the truth.

Despite the *appearance* of kindness, the truth could be told in the way a man ordered his flowers.

These ones for Heather for example. It was the third time he'd ordered flowers for her. That would make this the make-up bouquet. He'd probably forgotten lunch or left her in the lurch at the opera. Perhaps a few asters, which signified an afterthought, mixed with the snap-dragons and roses.

If he followed his pattern, and there was no reason to believe he would not, there would be one more delivery of flowers—the-nice-knowing-you-bouquet—and then Heather would be history, along with the dozen or so others that Dylan had romanced.

A dozen women in a year. That was one a month. It was disgraceful.

And then there were the girls who waited in the wings, who received the occasional bouquet when lust-of-the-month was cooling: Tara, Sarah, Janet, and Margot. Add to that there was a special someone he chose flowers for himself, every Friday without fail.

Sending his flowers was like having a rather embarrassing personal look at his little black book!

It was absolutely shameful, Katie thought, that she could see through that man so clearly, despise his devil-may-care attitude with women, and still run to the window every day to watch the pure poetry of him running, still feel herself blush when he smiled at her or teased her, still feel that disastrous sense of *yearning* that had always meant nothing but trouble in her well-ordered life.

Dylan McKinnon walked through his office doors, checked his watch. A mile in six and a half minutes. Not bad for a guy about to turn twenty-seven. Not bad at all. His pulse was already back to normal.

He glanced around the reception area with satisfaction. The decor was rich and sensuous, deep-brown leather sofas, a genuine Turkish rug, good art, low lighting. A pot of Katie's flowers, peach-colored roses that seemed to glow with an inner light, was on the reception desk. All in all, he thought his office was not too bad for a guy who had not even finished college.

"Could you call Erin in design?" he said to the receptionist. "Just tell her I think we should consider making the hood on this jacket removable before it goes into production." What about zip-on sleeves, since by *definition* a jacket had sleeves? "Actually, have her call me."

"All right," the receptionist said.

Margot was a gorgeous girl; married, thankfully. He did not date women who were married or who worked for him, clearly demonstrating what an ethical guy he was, something that would surprise the hell out of Katie, the flower girl.

Dylan shook off the little shiver of unexpected regret he felt. What did he care if Katie's disapproval of him telegraphed through her ramrod-stiff spine every time he walked in her store? It was *entertaining,* he told himself sternly. He'd thought, once or twice, of asking her out—he knew from casual conversations over the year he'd known her, she was single, and something about her intrigued—but she was way more complicated than the kind of girl he liked.

The receptionist apologetically handed him a ream of pink message slips. "One from your dad, one from your sister," she said. "The rest from Miss Richards."

"Ah," he said, and stuffed them in his pocket. He didn't want to talk to his dad today. Probably not tomorrow, either. As for Heather, okay, so he'd missed her last night. She'd wanted him to go to a fashion show. Real men didn't go to fashion shows. He'd implied he *might* attend to avoid sulking or arguments, but he'd never promised he would accompany her. Apparently he had only postponed the inevitable.

He'd gotten in from the sports pub that he was a part owner of to see his answering machine blinking in a frenzy. Each message from her; each one more screechy than the last.

Heather was beginning to give him a headache. Right on schedule. How come girls like Heather always acted like, well, Heather? Possessive, high maintenance, predictable.

Predictable.

That's what he was to Katie, the flower lady. He didn't really know whether to be annoyed or amused that she had his number so completely.

Still, how had she known what to write on that card for Heather?

The little minx was psychic. And darned smart. And hilariously transparent. He had thought she was going to faint when he'd nearly taken his jacket off in front of her. She had a quality of naïveté about her that was refreshing. Intriguing. She'd told him once, tight-lipped and reluctant to part with anything that might be construed as personal information, that she was divorced. Funny, for someone who had "forever girl" written all over her.

The fact that he was predictable to someone who was a little less than worldly, despite her divorce, was somewhat troubling.

Rather than be troubled, he picked the least of the three evils on his messages and called Tara.

"Hey, sis," he said when she answered. "How are you?" He could hear his fourteen-month-old nephew, Jake, howling in the background.

Tara, never one for small talk, said, "Call Dad, for Pete's sake. What is wrong with you?"

His sister was seven years older than him. He had long-ago accepted that she was never going to look at him as a world-class athlete or as Hillsboro's most successful entrepreneur. She was just going to see her little brother, who needed to be bullied into doing what was right. What she perceived was right.

"And for heaven's sake, Dylan, who is that woman you are being photographed with? A new low, even for you. Miss Hillsboro Mud Wrestler? Sheesh."

"She is not Miss Hillsboro Mud Wrestler!" he protested. Only his sister would see a girl like Heather as a new low. The guys at Doofus's Pub knew the truth. Heather was *hot*.

"Dylan, call Dad. And find a decent girl. Oh, never mind. I doubt if you could find a decent girl who would go out with you. Honestly, you are too old to be a captive of your hormones, and too young to be having a midlife crisis. Mom's sick. She isn't going to get any better, and you can't change that by racing your motorcycle or dating every bimbo in Hillsboro. And beyond."

"I'm not trying to change anything," he said coolly indignant.

"Humph," she said with disbelief.

Don't ask her, he ordered himself, but he asked anyway, casually, as if he couldn't care less. "How would you define decent?"

"Wholesome. Sweet. *Smart* would be a nice change. I have to go. Jake just ate an African violet. Do you think that's poisonous?"

I'm sure it's nothing compared to your tongue. He refrained from saying it. "Bye, sis."

"Only someone who loves you as much as me would tell you the truth."

"Thanks," he said dryly.

Still, as he hung up, he reluctantly recognized the gift of her honesty. Too many people fawned over him, but refreshingly, his sister was not one of them.

And neither was Katie Pritchard, who, when he thought about it, was the only woman he knew who even remotely would fit his sister's definition of *decent*.

He ordered a ton of flowers from her, even before someone told him she sent secret messages in with the blossoms. But so far not one person on the receiving end had said a single word about secret messages.

Still, despite the lack of secret messages, he liked going into her little shop. It was like an oasis in the middle of the city. Perversely, he *liked* it that while she could barely contain her disapproval of him she still nearly fainted when he threatened to do something perfectly normal, like remove his jacket.

He liked bugging her. He liked *sparring* with her. Okay, in the past year he had played with the fact most women found him, well, irresistible, but not nearly on the level he had Katie believing. He'd taken to going in there when he was bored and sending flowers to his sister. Also on the receiving end of bouquets were his PR manager, Sarah, and Sister Janet, the nun who ran the boys and girls club. Sometimes Dylan ordered flowers just to see Katie's lips twitch with disapproval when he said, "Just put 'From Dylan with love.'" Even the flowers on the reception desk right now had arrived with that card, addressed to Margot, which he'd quickly discarded.

And, of course, once a week, he went in and she let him go into the refrigerated back room and pick out his own bouquet from the buckets of blossoms there. She would never admit it, but he knew no one else was allowed into that back room. He never told her anything about that bouquet, or who it was for, and Katie did not ask, but probably assumed the worst of him.

Katie found him predictable. Katie, who looked as if she was trying out for librarian of the year.

Every time she saw him, she put those glasses on that made her look stern and formidable. And the dresses!

Just because she was the flower girl, did that mean there was some kind of rule that she had to wear flowered dresses, the kind with lace collars, and that tied at the back? She had curves under there, but for some reason she had decided not to be attractive. She wore flat black shoes, as if she was ashamed of her height, which he thought was amazing. Didn't she know models were tall and skinny, just like her? Okay, most of them had a little more in the chest department, but at least hers looked real.

It all added up to one thing. *Decent.*

He smiled evilly, wondering how the flower girl would feel if she knew he had covertly studied her chest and pronounced it authentic?

She'd probably throw a vase of flowers right at his head.

At the thought of little Miss Calm and Cool and Composed being riled enough to throw something, Dylan felt the oddest little shiver. Challenge? He'd always been a man who had a hard time backing down from a challenge.

His sister had said a decent girl wouldn't go out with him. So much easier to focus on that than to think about the other things Tara had said, or about calling his father. Besides if a decent girl would go out with him that would make Tara wrong about everything.

Why not Katie? He'd always been reluctantly intrigued by her, even though she was no obvious beauty. She was cute, in that deliberately understated way of hers, and he realized he liked her hair: light brown, shiny, wisps of it falling out of her ponytail. Still, she *could* smile more often, wear a dusting of makeup to draw some attention to those amazing hazel eyes, but no, she *chose* to make herself look dowdy.

She did fit his sister's definition of decent. Wholesome she was. And smart? He was willing to bet she knew the name of the current mayor of Hillsboro, and who the prime minister of Canada was, too. She would know how to balance her checkbook, where to get the best deal on toilet paper—though if you even mentioned toilet paper around her she would probably turn all snooty—and the titles of at least three Steinbeck novels.

He was just as willing to bet she wouldn't know a basketball great from a hockey sensation. He liked how she seemed unsettled around him, but did her darnedest to hide it. He was pretty sure she watched him run every day.

So, Katie thought he was predictable? So, his Tara didn't think a decent girl would go out with him?

If there was one thing Dylan McKinnon excelled at it was being unpredictable. It was doing the unexpected. It was taking people by surprise. That was what had made him a superb athlete and now an excellent businessman. He always kept his edge.

His phone rang. It was the receptionist.

"Heather on the line."

"I'm not here."

He'd talk to Heather after she got her flowers. That should calm her down enough to be reasonable. There had been a hockey game on TV last night. No one in their right mind would have expected him to go to a fashion show instead of watching hockey. It was nearly the end of the season!

Heather had promised him girls modeling underwear, but the truth was he didn't care. He was growing weary of his own game.

Secretly, he didn't care if he never saw one more woman strutting around in her underwear again. One more top that showed a belly button, or one more pair of figure-hugging jeans. He didn't care if he never saw one more body piercing, one more head of excruciatingly blond hair, one more set of suspiciously inflated breasts.

He felt like a man trying to care about all the things the wealthy successful businessman ex-athlete was supposed to care about, but somehow his sister was right. He wasn't outrunning anything. His heart wasn't in it anymore. He wanted, no, yearned for something different. He wanted to be *surprised* for a change, instead of always being the one surprising others.

He thought of her again, of Katie, of those enormous hazel eyes, intelligent, wary, behind those glasses.

On an impulse he picked up the phone, rolled through his Rolodex, punched out her number.

"The Flower Girl."

"Hey, Katie, my lady, Dylan."

Silence.

Then, ever so politely, "Yes?"

"Would you—" What was he doing? Had he been on the verge of asking her out for dinner? Katie, the flower girl? He felt an uncharacteristic hesitation.

"Yes?"

"Uh, name three Steinbeck novels for me? I'm doing a questionnaire. I could win a prize. A year's worth of free coffee from my favorite café." He lied with such ease, another talent that Katie would disapprove of heartily.

"You don't know the names of three of Steinbeck's novels?" she asked, just a hint of pity in her cool voice.

"You know. Dumb jock."

"Oh." She said, as if she *did* know, as if it had completely slipped her mind—or it didn't count—that he ran a multi-million-dollar business. "Which ones would you like? The most well-known ones? The first ones? Last ones?"

"Any old three."

"Hmm. *East of Eden. The Grapes of Wrath. Of Mice and Men.* Though, personally, I'd have to say I think his finest work was a short story called 'The Chrysanthemums.'"

He laughed. "That figures. About flowers, right?"

"About an unhappy marriage."

"Is there any other kind?" he asked, keeping his tone light. In actual fact, his parents had enjoyed an extraordinary union—until unexpectedly the "worse" part of the better-or-worse equation had hit and his father had turned into a man Dylan didn't even know.

She was silent, and he realized he'd hit a little too close to home, a reminder of why he couldn't ever ask her out. She was sensitive and sweet, and he was, well, not.

And then she said, softly, with admirable bravery given the fact she had presumably not had a good marriage, at all, "I like to hope."

Oh-oh! A girl who liked to hope, despite the fact divorce was part of her history. Still, if she *hoped* you'd think she'd try just a little harder to *attract.*

"Not for myself personally," she added, her voice suddenly strangled. "I mean, I just want to believe, somewhere, somehow, someone is happy. Together. With another someone."

He snorted, a sound redolent with the cynicism he had been nurturing for the past year.

The word *hope* used in any conversation pertaining to marriage should be more than enough to scare any devoted bachelor near to death, but he'd always had trouble with risk assessment once he'd set a challenge for himself.

If anything, a jolt of fear sent him forward rather than back. That was why Dylan had skied every black diamond run at Whistler Blackcomb. He had bungee-jumped off the New River Gorge Bridge in Virginia on Bridge Day. He planned to sign up for a tour on the Space Shuttle the first year his company grossed five hundred million dollars. Dylan McKinnon prided himself in the fact he was afraid of nothing. He'd *earned* the nickname "Daredevil."

He took chances. That's why he was where he was today.

It was also the reason his baseball career had ended almost before it started, the voice of reason tried to remind him.

He overrode the voice of reason, took a deep breath, spat it out. "Would you like to go for dinner sometime?"

Silence.

"Katie? Are you there?"

"You haven't even sent the fourth bouquet to Heather yet," she said.

"The what?"

"The fourth one. The nice-to-know-you-I'm-such-a-great-guy-I'm-sending-flowers-but-I'm-moving-on one."

He felt a shiver go up and down his spine. How was it that Katie knew him so well? He thought of the year he had known her, those intelligent eyes scrutinizing him, missing nothing. Assessing, mostly correctly, that he was a self-centered, selfish kind of guy.

"Okay," he said. "Send it. Instead of the I'm-sorry one."

"I already sent that one."

Little Miss Efficient. "Okay, send the other one, too, then."

"Do you want the message to read, 'It's been great knowing you. I wish you all the best'?"

He *had* become predictable. Hell. "Sure," he said, "That's fine."

"Anything else?"

"You tell me. Am I available now that the fourth bouquet is being sent?"

"Of course you are," she said sweetly.

Sweet had been one of the components his sister had used to define decent.

"Great. When would you like to go for dinner?"

"Never," she said firmly.

He was stunned, but he realized there was only one reason little miss Katie Wholesome would have said no to him. And it wasn't what his sister had said, either, that no decent girl would go out with him!

"You have a guy, huh?"

Pause. "Actually, I have a customer. If you'll excuse me." And then she hung up. Katie Pritchard hung up on him.

He set down the phone, stunned. And then he began to laugh. Be careful what you wish for, he thought. He'd wished for a surprise, and she had delivered him one.

He'd just been rejected by Katie, the flower girl. He should have been fuming.

But for the first time in a long time he felt challenged. He could make her say *yes*.

Then what, he asked himself? A funny question for a man who absolutely prided himself in *not* asking questions about the future when it came to his dealings with the opposite sex.

Despite the rather racy divorcée title, Katie would be the kind of girl who didn't go out with a guy without a chaperone, a written contract and a rule book. The perfect girl to invite to dinner at his sister's house. That was the *then what,* and nothing beyond that.

So why did his mind ask, *What would it be like to kiss her?*

"Buddy," he told himself, "what are you playing with?"

For some reason, even though she was pretending to be the plainest girl in Hillsboro, he could picture her lips, *exactly*. They were wide and plump, and even without a hint of lipstick on them, they practically begged a man to taste them.

He tried to think what Heather's lips looked like. All he could think of was red grease smeared on his shirt collar. He shuddered, even though Heather was not a girl who would normally make a man shudder.

"Playing with Katie is like toying with a saint," he warned himself. But he was already aware that he felt purposeful. Katie intrigued him, and he wanted her to come out for dinner with him. He was also about to prove to his sister how wrong she could be. About everything.

Now, how was he going to convince Katie to go out with him? He bet it wouldn't be hard at all. If he applied a little pressure to that initial resistance, she'd cave in to his charm like an old mine collapsing.

An old mine collapsing, he told himself happily. *Take that, Steinbeck.*

CHAPTER TWO

"NEVER!" Katie repeated, slamming down the phone and glaring at it.

What had that been all about, anyway? Whatever it was, she hadn't liked it one little bit. Why was Dylan McKinnon asking her out?

To be completely honest, it was a moment she had fantasized about since she had moved in next door to him, but like most fantasies, when it actually happened, the collision with reality was not pretty. Going out with him would *wreck* everything.

Because he only went out with people temporarily.

And then it would be over. Really over. No more Dylan dropping by her shop to tease her, to order flowers, to ruffle her feathers, to remind her of the fickleness of men. Dylan, without her really knowing it, had helped take her mind off the death of her marriage.

The death of—she stopped herself. She was not thinking about that death.

Two years since she and Marcus had parted ways. In the past year, the flower shop had given her a sense of putting her life back together. Whether she liked it or not, Dylan had been part of that.

It occurred to her that if Dylan's running by her window and unexpected drop-bys had become such a highlight in her life, she really had allowed herself to become pathetic.

As if to underscore that discovery, she suddenly caught a glimpse of herself in the mirror—no makeup, hair drawn back in a careless ponytail, and that dress. It was truly hideous, and she knew it. But when she had opened The Flower Girl she had convinced herself to take on a persona, she had shopped for vintage dresses that would underscore the image she was trying to create: back-to-nature, wholesome, flower child.

But underneath she was aware of another motive. Fear. She didn't want to be attractive anymore. She wanted to protect herself from all the things that being attractive to men meant.

It meant being asked out. Participating in the dance of life. It might mean a heart opening again, hope breathing back to life.

I like to hope, she had foolishly said to Dylan.

But the truth was the last thing she wanted was to *hope.* Ever since the breakup of her parents' marriage when she was nine, she had dreamed of a little house and her own little family. Dreamed of a bassinet and a sweet-smelling baby—

Katie slammed the door on those thoughts. Dylan had asked her out for dinner, and already some renegade part of herself wanted to *hope.* She congratulated herself on having the strength to say no before it went one breath further.

As egotistical as he was, even Dylan McKinnon had to understand *never.*

She sighed. Dylan was a disruptive force in the universe. The female part of the universe. Specifically, her part of the universe.

She glanced at the clock. Close enough to quitting time to shut the doors. She closed up and made a decision to head to a movie. Distract herself with something like a political thriller that had nothing to do with romance, love, babies. All those things that could cut so deeply.

But, as she was leaving her business, so was he. Despite her effort to turn the lock more quickly, pretend she didn't see him, *escape,* her fingers were suddenly fumbling, and there he was looking over her shoulder.

"Hey," he said, taking the keys from her, turning the lock, handing them back, "I think we're going to redesign the jacket."

She was annoyed that she had to see him again so soon after declaring *never,* and even more annoyed that she shivered with awareness at that brief touch of his hand. Still, she could be relieved that he seemed to have already forgotten he had asked her out. That's how much it had meant to him.

"Make the hood detachable, sleeves that zip on."

He was too close to her; she liked the protection of her counter separating them. The cool scent of mountain breezes wafted from him, his eyes were intent on hers. She struggled to know what he was talking about, and then realized he was back to the jacket she had seen him running in. She didn't care about his jacket. She wanted to get away from him. Desperately. How dare he look so glorious without half trying? How dare he make her so aware she was looking a little frumpy today? How dare he make her care, when she had managed to care about so little for so long?

"I don't like clothes with zip-on parts," she said, then instantly regretted offering her opinion, when it did not forward her goal of getting away.

He frowned at her. "Why not?"

"Because they're confusing and hard to use," she said.

He eyed her. "You're not particularly coordinated. Remember the time you dropped the vase of roses? Slipped on the ice out there, and I had to help you up? Or how about the time you tripped over that piece of carpet and went flying?"

His eyes crinkled at the corners when he smiled. He was aging, just like everybody else. So, he was the one other man in the universe, besides Richard Gere, who could make eye crinkles look sexy.

"Thank you for bringing up all of my happier memories," she said, annoyed. It was really unfair that he could make her feel as embarrassed as if that had happened yesterday. Of course, he never had to know it was him who brought about that self-conscious awkwardness!

"So, no offense, but you're not exactly the person we're designing for."

"That's too bad," she said, coolly, "because I'm average, just like most of the people who buy your clothing are average. They're going for a run around the block, or taking their dog out for a walk. They want to look athletic, but it doesn't necessarily mean they are. They aren't getting ready for the Olympics or the Blue Jays training camp."

He was glowering at her, which was so much better than the sexy eye-crinkle smile, so she continued.

"So, then it starts raining, and where are your sleeves and your hood if they're detachable? Making nice lumps in your pockets? Or at home on the entryway table? Within three months I would have lost at least one of the sleeves, and probably the hood."

He sighed. "We need you on the design team. Want a job?"

"No."

"Okay, want to go grab a burger, then?"

She eyed him narrowly. Ridiculous to think he had given up on his dinner invitation. He had the innocent look down pat, but when he wanted something, she was willing to bet he had the tenacious predator spirit of a shark! "I already told you no to dinner."

"Grabbing a burger is not exactly dinner," he said. "Market research. The smartest girl I know can help me with my jacket design."

"I am not the smartest girl you know!" Oh boy, relegated to the position of the smart one. Almost as dreadful as being relegated to the position of a friend but never a girlfriend.

"Yup, you are."

"Well then you don't know very many girls."

"We both know that's a lie," he said smoothly.

"Okay, you don't know very many girls who hang out at the library instead of at Doofus's Pub and Grill."

"You don't have to say that as if it's a dirty word. I'm a part owner in Doofus's."

Which explained why a place with a name like Doofus's could be so wildly successful. The man had the

Midas touch—not that she wanted to weaken herself any further by contemplating his touch. She had to be strong.

Hard, with him gazing at her from under the silky tangle of his soot-dark eyelashes. "Do *you* hang out at the library?" he asked.

How could he say that in a tone that made her feel as if he'd asked something way too personal, like the color of her underwear. She could feel an uncomfortable blush starting. "You don't have to say *that* as if it's a dirty word. The library is beautiful. Have you ever been to the Hillsboro Library?"

"Have you ever been to Doofus's?" he shot back.

"Oh, look," she said, changing the subject deftly, "it's starting to rain. And me without my zip-on sleeves. I've got to go, Dylan. See you at the library sometime."

But his hand on her sleeve stopped her. It was not a momentous occasion, a casual touch, but it was the second one in as many minutes. But given she had not wanted to even *think* about his touch, it seemed impossibly cruel that she now was experiencing it again. He probably touched people—girl people—like that all the time. But the easy and unconscious strength in his touch, the sizzle of heat, made her heart pound right up into her throat, made her feel weak and vulnerable, made her ache with a treacherous longing.

"Tell me something about you," he said. "One thing. Anything you want."

"I just did. I like the library." No wonder he had a woman a month! When he said that, his eyes fastened on her face so intently, it felt as if he really wanted to know! She *knew* it was a line, so she hated herself for feeling honored by his interest.

"Something else," he said.

"I live with three males," she said, no reason to tell him they were cats.

He laughed. "I bet they're cats."

The thing you had to remember about Dylan McKinnon was that underneath all that easygoing charm, he was razor sharp. She glanced down at herself to see if had completed her glamorous look today with cat hair, but didn't, thankfully, see any.

"I'm divorced," she reminded him, hoping that failure would be enough to scare him off, unless he enjoyed the horrible stereotype some men had of a divorced woman, a woman who had known the pleasures of the marital bed, and now did not: *hungry.*

"That is a surprise about you," he said. "I would have never guessed divorced."

Had she succeeded in making herself look so frumpy that he didn't believe anyone would have married her? If that was true, what was his sudden interest in her?

"Why not?" she demanded.

"I don't know. You seem like a decent girl."

"Divorced women are indecent?" she asked, and then found herself blushing, looking furiously away from him.

"Sorry." He touched her chin. He had to quit touching her! "I didn't mean it like that. You just seem like the kind of woman who would say forever and mean it."

"I did mean it!" she said, with far more feeling than she would have liked.

"So it was his fault."

She was not going to have this way-too-intimate conversation with Dylan McKinnon on a chance meeting on a public street.

"Does it have to be somebody's fault?" she asked woodenly. Who, after all, could predict how people would react to tragedy? She had miscarried the baby she wanted so badly. It had all unraveled from there.

Sometimes, when she couldn't sleep at night, she tormented herself by wondering if it had been unraveling already, and if she had hoped the baby would somehow glue it back together, give her someone to love in the face of a husband who was distant, from a life that was so far from the fairy tale she had dreamed for herself. This was exactly why she now dedicated her life to her business. Business was not *painful*. It did not cause introspection. It did not leave time for self-pity or self-analysis.

"Come grab a burger with me at Doofus's," he said, and laid a persuasive hand on her wrist.

She heard something gentle in his voice, knew she had not succeeded in keeping her pain out of her eyes.

"They make a mean burger."

"I'm a vegetarian."

"Really?" he said skeptically.

"If I went there, would you come to the library after?" she said, sliding her arm out from under his touch as if she was making a sneak escape from a cobra. Maybe the best defense was an offense. He'd be about as likely to visit a library as she would be to visit a turkey shoot. Still, as he contemplated her, her heart was acting as if she was in a position of life-threatening danger, racing at about thirteen million beats per minute.

"Sure. I'll come to the library. I *like* doing different things. Surprising myself."

Right. He just had all the answers. He'd never go to

the library, just say he was going to, and then send a bouquet of flowers when he didn't show.

"Why are you doing this?" she asked, folding her rescued limbs over her chest, protectively.

He sighed, looked away, ran a hand through the rich darkness of his hair. "I want a change," he said, and she was pretty sure he surprised them both with his sincerity.

Still, to be asked out because he needed a change from his bevy of bimbos? It was insulting!

"And you'd like a new toy to play with," she guessed, with a shake of her head.

He regarded her thoughtfully. "I bet your husband didn't deserve you. He probably wasn't worth the sadness I saw in your eyes when you mentioned your divorce."

The comment was unexpected, his voice quiet and serious, a side of him she had never seen.

Dylan McKinnon's charm was dangerous when he was all playful and boyish. But it turned downright lethal when he became serious, the cast of his face suddenly accentuating the firmness around his mouth, the strength in the cut of his cheekbones and chin.

"I have to go," she said.

She whirled away from him. Her eyes were stinging.

"Hey, Katie," he said, jogging up beside her now, blocking her attempt to escape from all his sympathy with some dignity, "I'm sorry, I didn't mean to hurt you."

"Would you go away? Guys like you always hurt girls like me."

He stopped. Stared at her. She saw her arrow had hit.

"Not every man is going to be like your ex-husband," he said evenly.

"How do you know? You didn't know him." *Or me.*

The truth was it didn't really matter if Dylan was like Marcus, if she was still like her. It was herself she didn't trust after her whole life had fallen apart. She did not trust herself to make good choices, and certainly not to be able to survive that kind of pain ever again.

But it was true Dylan was nothing like Marcus had been. Dylan had his faults, but he didn't try to hide any of them. If anything, he seemed to celebrate them. He didn't seem to have any secrets, unless she counted that one bouquet that he picked himself every week and delivered himself.

Other than that her remark about guys like him hurting girls like her was really undeserved. He had been her most loyal customer. He'd always only been kind to her, funny and charming. He'd helped her pick up the glass that time she had broken the rose vase. He had a gift for making her feel oddly pretty—or at least interesting—even on her ugliest days. He was aggravatingly sure of himself, yes, but he never crossed that line into conceit.

"Come have a hamburger," he said. "No strings attached. I promise I'll make you laugh."

"How can you promise that?" she said, aware suddenly that she *ached* to laugh. To feel light and unburdened. To forget that she had failed at marriage and miscarried a baby. In his eyes she thought she glimpsed something of herself she had lost, a woman who had been carefree and laughter filled. She longed, suddenly, to be that woman again, even if only for a little while.

The pull of being returned to a happier self was too strong to resist.

"Okay," she said, "A hamburger. To reassure you that

I'm not in any danger of turning into a tragic cat lady. And maybe to give you a few ideas for a jacket that people won't lose the sleeves of. And then that's the end of this. Am I clear?"

He nodded with patent insincerity.

She looked at her watch. She could make a quick trip to the mall before she met him. If sympathy had in any way motivated this invitation, there would be nothing like a new pair of jeans and a slinky top to convince him—and herself—that she was not in need of it.

"I'll meet you. In an hour. At Doofus's."

"Perfect," he said, and smiled that slow, sexy utterly sincere smile that had convinced a zillion women before her they were the only one that mattered to him.

It was once she was safe in her car, away from the mesmerizing magnetism of him, that she allowed herself to look hard at the terrible truth he did not know…or maybe he did.

She had a crush on him! That was why she watched him run every day! Look at how easily he had overcome her objections! She had vowed one moment she was never going out to dinner with him, and broken that vow within minutes of having made it.

"I can't do this," she realized.

Because what if—okay it was way out there—but what if they developed feelings for each other? What if she fell in love with him, and he with her? What if all her fairy-tale fantasies roared back to life?

And what if she lost *again?*

"I cannot survive another loss," she whispered. So much safer to have an unrealistic crush on a man, to watch him run, to keep a safe enough distance that each of his faults remained crystal clear, not blurred by the beauty of his physique, his eyes, the totally unexpected firmness in his voice, when he'd said, "I bet he didn't deserve you."

No. Here was the thing she was going to have to realize with her and with men, whether it was Marcus Pritchard, who had seemed safe and stable, or Dylan McKinnon, who seemed dangerous, but who called to some part of her that wanted an adventure. Her judgment was just plain bad.

Some people had good instincts. They knew good people from bad, they knew which horse to bet on, they got a chill up and down their spine if the airplane they were about to board was going to crash.

Katie did not consider herself one of those people. Not anymore. The girl most likely to stay married forever was now divorced. Following her heart the first time had led her to heartbreak. But had it been her heart she had followed, or a desperate need to believe in family after her own had broken apart?

She wanted to impress Dylan that she could look great in hip-hugging jeans and tops that showed a little décolleté? She had to fight that impulse and do the exact opposite! She didn't need to upgrade her wardrobe! She needed to downplay it even more than it was downplayed now.

So, instead of driving to the mall, she drove home. Her three cats, Motley, Crew, and Bartholomew greeted her at the door with enthusiasm that could have only been earned by a tragic cat person.

Though it was still early, she reached way into the back of her closet, found her ugliest, frumpiest and most comfortable flannel pajamas. She heated a frozen pizza in the microwave and finally looked up the number of Doofus's.

"Is Dylan McKinnon there?"

"Who's asking?"

The question said it all. It was asked warily, as if the bartender fielded dozens of these calls. Women, infatuated beyond pride, beyond reason, calling for Dylan, after hearing he hung out there.

"Um, I was supposed to meet him there in a few minutes. Could you tell him I can't make it?"

"You're standing up Dylan McKinnon? Who are you? Leticia Manning?"

The mention of the young and very gorgeous Canadian actress served as a reminder of the kind of woman Dylan *really* went out with, the status of the kind of women he really went out with. Katie Pritchard was a plain Jane. He was a playboy. She needed to remember that.

"Unless he's expecting more than one woman to meet him tonight—" a possibility? "—he'll know who I am!" she said, slammed down the phone, and took a bite of her pizza. It tasted exactly like cardboard. Bartholomew climbed on her lap and she broke off a piece and fed it to him. He purred and sighed and kneaded her with his paws.

Which begged the question—what was so wrong with being a crazy cat lady? She'd send Dylan a bouquet of flowers tomorrow by way of apology. After all, he did it all the time.

Dylan took a sip of his beer, put the nine ball in the side pocket and glanced at the door. The smug sense of self-congratulation that he had felt ever since he'd so easily changed her mind about coming here was dissipating. Was she coming or not? He was a little unsettled by how tense he felt now that it was getting later and she wasn't here. Katie was not the "fashionably late" kind of gal. It was raining quite hard now. The streets would be slick. Did her lack of coordination extend to her driving? Had she—

"Hey, boss," Cy called, "your lady friend ain't coming. She just called."

Rafe Miller looked up from the pool table, guffawed with great enjoyment. "Hey, Dill, you been stood up!"

Dylan liked coming to Doofus's because it was just a local watering hole. It was staffed by people he'd known for a long time. Most of the clients were his buddies. No one here was the least impressed with his celebrity, which at the moment, for one of the first times in his memory, he was sorry for. Guys who really knew you had no respect; they didn't know when to back off.

"Are you seeing Leticia Manning?" Cy asked.

More guffaws.

Dylan glared at him.

"Because she was snooty sounding, just like Leticia Manning."

Well, that left absolutely no question about who had called.

"Want me to cancel your burger?" Cy said helpfully.

"Hell, no." That would make it too much like he cared. And he didn't. Though when he'd seen that pain flash through her eyes at the mention of her divorce, he had cared, for a second. He had sincerely wanted to make her laugh, not just prove to his sister—and himself—that a decent girl would so go out with him.

Then there was the possibility she was teaching him a little lesson. She'd been sending his flowers too long. She knew he stood people up sometimes. She knew he'd let down Heather last night. It would be just like Katie to want him to know how it felt.

And the truth was it didn't feel very good.

Tonight he'd been the one who had learned something, whether she'd intended it or not. It didn't feel too good to be the one left waiting. Dumped. Stood up. Imagine Katie Pritchard being the girl who taught him that!

But he doubted Katie was trying to teach him anything. She was terrified, plain and simple. Marriage had burned her.

He thought of his parents. Maybe marriage burned everyone, given enough time. Which was why, for the past year, he'd been intent on not getting serious, not committing, not caring. Katie needed to learn just that. You could still live, without risking your heart. He bet he could have made her laugh. He bet he could show her laughing again didn't have to mean hurting again.

If he was so determined to tangle his life with hers a little more deeply it occurred to him it was going to require more of him than he had required of himself before. He would actually have to think a bit about her, not just about himself. He would have to be a better man.

Right there at Doofus's, with the tang of beer in the air, and pool balls clacking, Dylan McKinnon had an epiphany.

This is what his sister had tried to tell him: that he could be more. That he had not expected enough of himself. That to get a decent girl to even have dinner with him he had to be a decent man, someone capable of putting another person's interests ahead of his own, capable of venturing out of a place where he risked nothing.

His sister had seen a painful truth. Dylan McKinnon was known as being fearless. But in the area of caring about other people, he was not fearless at all.

He was not the man his mother would have wanted him to be.

So, it was a good thing Katie hadn't shown. Because that type of total attitude shift was the type of thing a man wanted to think about long and hard before he committed to it. Dylan didn't want to be a better man. He liked the man he was just fine. As far as erasing that flit of sorrow from the flower lady's eyes, he was the wrong man for the job.

"Rack 'em, Rafe. Cy, bring everyone a drink."

"What are we celebrating?" Cy asked, suspiciously.

"Freedom," Dylan said, remembering he'd ordered the kiss-off bouquet for Heather today, too.

That announcement was followed by some serious whistling and whooping.

But for all that he tried, and hard, to catch the mood of his own celebration, in the back of his mind a single word worried him.

Terrified.

And he just wasn't giving up on her that easily. Not even, damn it, if it did require that he be a better man.

The fact that a bright bouquet of flowers awaited him on his desk when he arrived the next morning only made him more determined. He flicked the card open.

"Sorry I couldn't make it last night, Love K."

Well, at least he'd taught her something in the year he'd known her!

He sat down and thought. Obviously, a burger at a sports bar had limited appeal to Katie. He'd always been able to count on his own appeal to convince women to take a leap out of their comfort zone, but Katie just wasn't most women. He needed a Plan B.

What would be irresistible to her? It was humbling to realize for Katie it was not him! Dylan McKinnon had become accustomed to being irresistible to women!

Whether she knew it or not, Katie had thrown down the gauntlet.

He was going to help her get back in the swing of things whether she liked it or not! To prove to his sister he could be a decent guy. Or maybe to prove it to himself.

By midafternoon he had two tickets to the most sought after event in Canada—the NHL All-Star hockey game.

He went into her store. She glanced up, looked back down hurriedly. She was blushing. "Sorry I couldn't make it last night. Something came up."

"What?"

She glared at him, annoyed he was rude enough to push. "Sanity."

He reminded himself, firmly, of his goal. One outing, or two, to make her feel attractive. Confident. *Happy*. To be who he guessed she once had been. He'd just help her get her feet wet again, so she didn't end up a tragic cat lady.

He guessed she had never been gorgeous, but lovely in some way that transcended whatever the current trend or fad was. She'd always had a way of holding herself that had seemed proud, as if she was above caring what others thought.

He'd just be a knight, for once in his life, show her

that she didn't have to roll over and die since her marriage had failed.

Looking at her, he realized she seemed to have worked extra hard at not being attractive today. The dress was billowing around her like a tent city, and her hair was pulled back a little too tightly from her face. Not a scrap of makeup, though now that he'd noticed her lips he realized she didn't really need it.

"Thanks for the flowers," he said.

"You were supposed to think it was funny."

"Ha-ha," he said.

She glared at him again. That was more like it, the green suddenly dancing to life in those multicolored eyes, snapping with color.

"So what can I do for you today?" she said. "Heather has been history for a full twelve hours or so. Someone else on the radar?"

If he told her she was on the radar, she'd run. He wouldn't catch her until Alaska, and then she'd probably throw herself into the Bering Sea and start swimming. It was an unusual experience for him to be having this kind of reaction from someone of the female persuasion.

"Um, no. I'm going to take a break for a while."

She was punching flowers into some sort of foam thing, but she lifted her eyes, looked at him, squinted.

"Uh-huh," she said, skeptical and not even trying to hide it.

"Here's what I was thinking. Maybe while I took a break, you could do a few things with me. Like the All-Star Game next weekend in Toronto."

Getting tickets to that game was like winning a

lottery, and he waited for her face to light up. Maybe she'd even come around the counter and give him a hug!

He was a little surprised by how much he would like to be hugged by Katie.

But instead of her face lighting up, she stabbed herself in the pad of her thumb with a rose thorn, glared at it, distracted.

"The what?" She stuck her thumb in her mouth and sucked. She really did not have to wear lipstick. Even watching her suck on that thumb was almost erotic. That was impossible! Look how the girl was dressed. He had just finished dating Miss Hillsboro Bikini, and never once felt the bottom falling out of his world like this.

Well, impossible or not, there was no denying how he was reacting.

"Haven't you got a Band-Aid?" he suggested, just a bit too much snap in his voice.

"Oh, it's just a little prick. They happen all the time. So, what kind of game is it you have tickets for?" she asked.

"Hockey," he said. Obviously she was in a completely different world than him if she didn't know that! "Canada's national game," he supplied when she looked blank. "Our passion, our pastime, our reason to be, during the long months of winter. You know the game?"

She took her thumb out of her mouth, thank goodness, went back to her flower arrangement. "Oh."

She wouldn't sound so unenthused if she knew what it took to get those tickets!

"The best players from the Western and Eastern Conferences get together and play each other. Every great player in the league on the ice at the same time." He began to name names.

She looked as if what he was discussing was about as interesting as choosing between steel-cut and quick cook oats for breakfast.

"Everybody wants tickets to that game," he snapped, feeling his patience begin to wane. He was being a knight, for goodness' sake. Why was she having such difficulty recognizing that?

"Oh," she said again, her vocabulary suddenly irritatingly limited.

"I could probably sell them on the Internet for a thousand bucks a pop."

"Oh, well then," she said, "don't waste them on me."

"It wouldn't be a waste," he sputtered. "You'd have fun. I guarantee it."

"You can't guarantee something like that!"

"Why is having a simple conversation with you like crossing a minefield?"

"Because I'm not blinking my eyelids at you with the devotion of a golden retriever?"

Well, there was that! "Katie, don't be impossible. I've got these great tickets to this great event. I know *in your heart* you want to say yes. Just say yes."

"You don't know the first thing about my heart."

Actually, he did. He'd seen a whole lot of things about her heart in one split second last night. That's why he was standing here trying so damned hard to be a decent guy. Obviously it was a bad fit for him. "That's what I mean about the minefield."

"Look, Dylan," she said with extravagant patience, as if he was a small child, "I know most girls would fall

all over themselves to do just about anything you suggested, including dogsled naked in the Yukon in the dead of winter, but I don't like hockey."

"Well, how do you feel about dogsledding naked, then?"

Ah, there was that blush again.

"Would you stop it? I don't want to go anywhere with you!"

"That hurts."

Oh, he saw that slowed her down a little bit: that he was a living breathing human being with feelings, not just some cavalier playboy.

But it only slowed her down briefly. "Don't even pretend my saying no would hurt you. Just go pick someone else out of your lineup of ten thousand hopefuls."

"I told you I'm taking a break."

"Well, I told you, not with me!"

"Give me one good reason!" he demanded.

"Okay. Going out with you is too public. I don't want my picture on the front page of the *Morning Globe,* I don't want the gossip columnist dissecting what I wear, and my hair."

"Then we'll go someplace private."

"No! Dylan, I don't want anything to change. I like the way my life is right now. You might think it looks dull and boring, but I like it."

There, he thought, he'd given it his best shot. He had tried to rescue the maiden in distress and failed. She had no desire to be rescued, he could go back to being superficial and self-centered, content in the knowledge he had tried.

She'd almost convinced him, but then he looked

more closely as she jabbed the last rose into the flower arrangement and managed to prick herself again.

She glanced at him, and looked quickly away.

And that's when he knew she was lying. She didn't prick herself all the time. She pricked herself when she was distracted.

She didn't like her life the way it was now. She'd settled. Katie really wanted all kinds of things out of life: dazzling things, things that made her heart beat faster, made her wake up in the morning and want to dance with whatever life offered that day.

She was afraid to hope.

And he was more determined than ever to give that back to her. But this was going to be the hard part, figuring out what was irresistible to her, not to him.

He walked back to his office, put the tickets on Margot's desk.

"Treat hubby to a night out," he said gruffly. Almost at his office he turned and looked back at her.

"And figure out what is the perfect date. Not for a guy. For a girl. What would be an absolutely irresistible outing to any woman? Ask your girlfriends. Get back to me."

His receptionist was looking at him as if he'd lost his mind. He stepped into his office and slammed the door.

Later, just to show Miss Snooty next door what she was missing in the excitement department, he got on his motorcycle and pulled a wheelie right in front of her window. Just in case she'd missed the first one, he went around the block and came back and did another one. Then just for good measure, he zipped back the other way.

As always, he was completely predictable to her.

The drapes of The Flower Girl were firmly closed.

CHAPTER THREE

KATIE could hear the sound of the motorcycle coming back down the street, the sudden change in engine pitch warning her Dylan was going to pop it up again.

She firmly closed the curtains.

Good grief! You would think no one had ever said no to that man. Of course, look at him. There was a chance, and a darn good one, that no one ever *had* said no to him. Or at least no one female!

And no wonder. It was not just hard to say no! A woman had to manually override all the biological and chemical systems in her entire body. And then, to add to the complexity of the task, she had to exercise steely control over her emotions.

Saying no to Dylan McKinnon was not fun and it was not easy. And he knew it! Imagine him leaning over that counter, dropping his voice a dreamy notch, looking straight into her eyes and saying as clearly as if he could see her soul, *I know, in your heart, you want to say yes.*

Of course she wanted to say yes! Thankfully she had a policy in place for dealing with him. In the interest of self-preservation, she had developed a new number-one rule: do exactly the opposite of what she *wanted* to do.

It was necessary. Her very survival felt as if it depended on saying no to him. For some reason she had shown up as a blip on Dylan McKinnon's radar. He had decided she *needed* something that he could give her.

But a hockey game? She considered hockey a barbaric, thinly disguised upgrade of the gladiator ring. Saying *yes* would be that first chip out of her soul: pretending she liked something she didn't to please him, becoming something other than what she was just to spend time at his side!

Even the way Dylan worded his invitation to attend that hockey game with him underscored the wisdom of her rejecting it. He was off women, but she'd do? He wanted a change, so she would be a slightly interesting distraction?

A girl just had to have some pride, and Katie knew that better than anyone. She knew how much pride you had to have to come to a small town after a failed marriage. And she knew she had a fragile hold on self-preservation. She could care about that man, and she simply did not want to. She had managed to put her life back together, barely, once, but she was pretty sure she couldn't do it again.

Still, the past year had made her privy to some important knowledge about Dylan. His passions were furious and frantic, but thankfully short-lived. As Hillsboro's most famous son, his every passing fancy, from motorcycle racing to whitewater rafting was carefully documented. He never stuck to anything for very long. He needed a fast pace, plenty of excitement, and if he didn't find them, he moved on. It was his modus operandi for life. From sending his flowers for the past year, Katie knew it was doubly true for the romantic part of his life.

He sent four bouquets during the course of a relationship. The first was his nice-to-meet-you, I'm-interested. The second, usually followed fairly closely on the heels of the first, and she was pretty sure it was the great-sex bouquet. Third, came the sorry-I-forgot, which he didn't really mean, and then the fourth was the goodbye bouquet. The cycle of a relationship that would probably take a normal person a year to play out—or at the very least a few months—he could complete in weeks.

Katie tried to sew warnings into the bouquets, bachelor buttons to signify celibacy for instance, but nobody paid the least bit of attention to the secret meanings of flowers these days, more's the pity.

There were two notable exceptions to Dylan's flower sending and his short attention span, one was the one bouquet he came in for once a week and chose himself.

He had never told her who it was for, but at some time she had let him start choosing his own flowers for it, even though her refrigerator room was sacred to her. Naturally, he had no idea of the meanings of what he was selecting, and yet he unerringly chose flowers like white chrysanthemums, which stood for truth, or daisies, which stood for purity and a loyal love. She never pressed about who the bouquet was for. His choice always seemed so somber, it did not seem possible it was a romantic bouquet.

The other exception to his short attention span was his business. In fact his drive, his restless nature, probably did him nothing but good when it came to running his wildly successful company, Daredevils.

He was constantly testing, developing and innovating. He loved the challenge of new products and new projects, which meant he was always on the cutting edge of business. He'd found the perfect line of work for his boundless energy. But those same qualities put him on the cutting edge of relationships, too, and not in a good way. He did the cutting!

The motorcycle roared by again, and against her better judgment she went and slid open one vertical pleat of her shades a half centimeter or so. He was wearing a distressed black leather jacket, jeans, no helmet. He looked more like a throwback to those renegades women always lost their hearts to—pirates and highwaymen—than Hillsboro's most celebrated success story.

Dylan gunned the bike to a dangerous speed, his silken dark hair flattened against his head, his eyes narrowed to a squint of pure focus. In a motion that looked effortless, he lifted the front wheel of that menacing two-wheeled machine off the ground. He made it rear so that he looked more like a knight on a rearing stallion than a perpetual boy with a penchant for black leather. For a moment he was suspended in time—reckless, strong, sure of himself—and then the front wheel crashed back to earth, he braced himself to absorb the impact and was gone down the street.

Dammit! She knew what he was doing was immature! Silly, even. Her head knew that! But her heart was beating hard, recognizing the preening of the male animal, reacting to it with a sheer animal longing of its own.

"I should call the police," she declared primly, even as she recognized her own lack of conviction. "I'm sure he's being dangerous. It's illegal not to wear a helmet."

That, she thought firmly, was just one more reason she had to say no to him. It was a classical and insurmountable difference between them. If she ever got on a motorcycle without a helmet, the anxiety of getting a head injury or getting a ticket would spoil it for her. Obviously it was taking chances that made the experience fun for him, that put him on the edge of pure excitement.

Here he came again, but instead of popping it up this time, he slowed down and pulled into a vacant parking spot outside her shop.

She ordered herself to drop the curtain, but was caught in the poetry of watching him dismount, throwing that long, beautiful leg up and over the engine.

She prayed he was going back to work, and not—

Her shop door squeaked open. She pretended a sudden intense interest in rearranging the flowers in the pot in the window, letting her hand rest on the white heather, which promised protection. But also could mean dreams come true. She hastily turned her attention to a different pot of flowers.

"Dark in here, Katie-my-lady."

She glanced at him, and then quickly away. She had to keep remembering his restless nature when he turned the full intensity of those blue eyes on her. Blue like sapphires, like deep ocean water, like every pirate and highwayman who had ridden before him.

"These flowers in the window were wilting. That's why I closed the drapes."

"Uh-huh."

"What do you want?"

"Play hooky with me," he said. "Come for a motorcycle ride."

One of the flowers snapped off in her hand. She stared at it. A pink carnation, rife with its multitude of meanings: fascination, a woman's love, I can't forget you, you are always on my mind.

She dropped the flower on the floor and stammered, "Are you crazy? You've just demonstrated to the whole neighborhood how you ride that thing!"

"Oh, were you watching? I could have sworn your drapes were closed."

It was like being caught red-handed at the cookie jar!

He bent and picked up the flower, smelled it, drawing its fragrance deep inside himself, his eyes never leaving hers. There was no way he could discern the secrets of that flower. He held it out to her, but she shook her head as if it was inconsequential, as if it meant nothing to her.

Absently, he threaded the carnation through the button hole of his leather jacket. How many men could do that with such casual panache? Wear a flower on their leather?

"We could cruise out of town," he said, just as if she had not refused him. "The fields are all turning green, the trees are budding. I bet we'd see pussy willows. Babies, too, calves and ducks, little colts and fillies trying out their long legs."

She could feel herself weakening, his voice a brush that painted pictures of a world she wanted to see. She knew spring was here: so many wonderful flowers becoming available locally, but somehow she had missed the *essence* of spring's arrival, its promise: gray and brown turning to green, plants long dormant bravely blooming again, sudden furious storms giving way to sunshine. It was the season of hope.

In fact, Dylan McKinnon was making her feel as if she had missed the essence of everything for a long, long time. He looked so good, standing there so full of confidence, the scent of leather in the air, his hair windswept, his eyes on her so intently.

She could almost imagine how it would feel to go with him, to feel the powerful purr of that bike vibrating through her, to wrap her arms tightly around his waist, to mold herself to his power and confidence, *feel* them, *feel* him in such an intoxicatingly intimate way.

"Say yes," he whispered. "You know you want to do something wild and crazy."

Yes. Yes. Yes.

"No!" The vow. Do the opposite of what she wanted. "I did something wild and crazy once. It involved saying yes, too. And it was a mistake."

They both knew she was referring to her marriage.

"You can't go through life without making mistakes, Katie."

"You can sure as hell try." It was because of his bad influence on her that she was using bad language. If she let this go any further, there was no telling what his influence would do. She would become a different woman than the one she was today.

She could picture herself with her head thrown back, laughing into the wind, while she clung to the motorcycle and him. Sensuous. Exhilarated. On fire with life. Willing to take chances.

Heartbroken! she snapped back at all those dreamy voices.

"Everybody makes mistakes, Katie. You learn from them, you let them make you better, and you move on."

"You with the charmed life!"

For a moment something so sad crossed his face that she was taken aback. But then he grinned, all devil-may-care charm again, and she could almost, but not quite, convince herself that she'd imagined it.

"What mistakes have you made?" she said. Oh, boy! She was getting sucked into this conversation when it was the last thing she wanted.

"Jumping out of an airplane a few months after signing my Blue Jays contract probably wasn't one of my more brilliant decisions," he said.

Was it that memory that had caused that brief sadness to chase across his features?

"So, why'd you do it?" All of Hillsboro still talked of his legendary jump. He'd agreed to do it as a fund-raiser for the local chapter of Big Brothers. Something had gone dreadfully wrong. He'd broken his arm in three places, ended his career as a pitcher before it had ever really even started. All of Hillsboro had gone into mourning over the misfortune of their most favored son.

He smiled. "I did it because I *wanted* to."

His lack of regret over the incident seemed to be genuine, but it proved exactly what she had already decided about *wanting*.

"Wanting is not a reliable compass with which to set the course of your life," she told him sternly. "You made an impulse choice that ruined your career."

He touched one of the flowers in the window, absently. Surprise, surprise, a red rose. *Passion*. His fingers caressed the petal with such tenderness that she could not help but wonder if it wouldn't be worth it. To give in. Just once. To give in to the impulse to play with the most dangerous fire of all: passion.

"You could look at it as an impulse choice that ruined my career," he agreed mildly. Thankfully, he decided to leave the rose alone. "I prefer to think a series of events played out that led me to my true calling."

She was startled by that. She had no awareness that he had moved on from his brush with fame without looking back, the same as he moved on with everything else. She shivered.

She didn't really want to know that about him. Nor did she want to start thinking about the events of her own life in ways that took down her protective barriers, instead of putting them up, in ways that made her more open to the vagaries of life, instead of battened down against them.

Mostly she didn't want to think about how that finger, tender on the petals of a rose, would feel if it brushed the fullness of her bottom lip.

Gathering all of her strength, she said, "I am not getting on that motorcycle with you. I like living!"

"Do you?" he asked softly, the faintest mocking disbelief in his tone. "Do you, Katie, my lady?" And with that, he turned on his heel and left her.

But the question he asked seemed to remain, burning deeper and deeper into her heart, her mind, her soul. *Did she?*

Did she like the nice safe predictable world she had created for herself? Were her flowers and her cats and her love of the library and her visits with her mother enough?

The road she had not taken teased her, the choice she had not made pulled at her, tantalized her, tormented her.

Katie could imagine how the wind would have felt in her face, the touch of sunlight on her cheeks. She could imagine laughter-filled moments, clinging to him on the back of his bike; relying on him to keep her safe. She felt intense regret for the courage she lacked.

She pulled herself to her senses. Ha, as if Dylan McKinnon could be relied on to keep anyone safe! Safe was the least likely word association that would come up in the same sentence as Daredevil Dylan McKinnon.

Then again, a little voice whispered to her, *maybe safety was entirely overrated.* She decided, uncaring of how childish it was, that she hated him.

Which, of course, was the safe choice. So much safer than loving him. Or anybody or anything else.

It occurred to her that if he had even noticed the hideousness of her outfit, it had not deterred him one little bit.

She had to do better. Tomorrow she was wearing her Indian cotton smock dress. And she'd look through that old trunk in the attic. She was sure there were flowered pink and green overalls in there. Of course, that was assuming he was dropping by again tomorrow, and in the days after that, too.

Considering she had decided she hated him, why was she looking forward to the possibility so much?

A charmed life, thought Dylan, hanging up the phone a few days later after his morning call to the nursing home. He contemplated Katie's assessment of him. In some ways it was so true. But he lived with another truth now.

He would trade it all—every single success he had ever enjoyed—to have one day to spend with his mother the way she used to be. After his mom's speedy decline into Alzheimer's, his father had made the unspeakable decision, last year, to put her in a home.

His grief was not just for his mother, but for the death of what he had believed. He had believed that someday he would have what his parents had, a quiet, steady kind of love that raised children and paid bills, that lived up to the vows they had taken, a love that stayed forever.

Instead his father, his model of what Dylan thought a man should be, had bailed.

His mother didn't even seem to know she had been betrayed. She was oblivious to her own illness, a blessing. The only thing that seemed to bring that spark to her eyes that Dylan remembered so well, were the flowers he brought her once a week. And then, only for the moment it took to name them, before the spark was gone, and she was looking at him blankly, as if to say, "Who are you?"

A knock on the door, Margot popped in.

"Sorry, a bad time?"

He had always disliked it when people could read him. It made him feel vulnerable. Margot was getting good at it. Katie had developed a disquieting gift for seeing through his fearless facade to what lay underneath. Maybe he should be remembering that when he was so intent on rescuing her, so intent on proving he could get a decent girl. That there might be a personal price to pay.

No, he was good at protecting himself. He proved it by grinning at Margot, seeing the faint worried crease on her forehead disappear with relief. "No, of course it's not a bad time," he assured her. He nodded toward his in-office basketball hoop. "I just missed a few. You know how I hate that."

"Here's the, er, research you asked me to do." Margot seemed uncharacteristically uncertain as she placed an untidy mountain of papers in front of him.

He didn't remember asking her to do any research, except maybe about the new running jacket. Puzzled, he picked up the first paper on the stack, and flinched. It had a title on it, like a high school essay. It said "My Dream Date with Dylan McKinnon."

Whatever he'd asked her for, Margot had misinterpreted it. Or maybe not. He couldn't remember exactly what he'd said to her.

Sheesh. Katie Pritchard had him rattled.

"Thanks," he said, and Margot looked pleased and left him alone with the monster he'd created.

Now because Katie had him rattled, Dylan's receptionist had presented him, pleased with herself, with a sheaf of papers from Lord knew where—girlfriends, acquaintances, women on the street—all of whom were just a little too eager to share highly personal information about themselves and what they liked to do in their spare time.

He looked at the stack of papers, rifled through. Tidy, messy, typed, printed, handwritten, perfumed. Someone extremely original had submitted her ideas written in red felt pen on a pair of panties. He disposed of the panties and wanted to just throw the rest of this self-created mess out, too.

But then again, there might be something in here—one small idea—that would help him unlock the fortress that was Katie.

He began to read the essay entitled My Dream Date

with Dylan McKinnon. Considering that it was quite neatly typed and double spaced, he wasn't ready for what it said. He was no prude, but he was shocked. He hastily crumpled up the paper and threw it in the garbage along with the panties.

Then he wondered if he should have done that. If he got any more frustrated with Katie, an evening with Ursula, a bottle of spray whipping cream, and a bed wrapped in plastic, might be a balm.

No, he left it in the garbage, reminded himself of the new *decent* Dylan, forced himself to read through the rest of the papers on his desk. Some of them had some ideas that were not half bad: a night at the ice hotel in Quebec, for one.

Not that he'd even think of asking Katie to spend the night with him, because she wasn't that kind of girl, but a *tour* of the ice hotel, and a few drinks of vodka out of ice mugs after the tour had a certain appeal. It was original, and what more perfect date for someone who was proving she could not be easily melted by his charms?

Plus, he liked the idea of feeding Katie a bit of vodka, straight up. He'd be willing to bet he could figure out what she was *really* thinking then.

The idea was taking hold, but then he looked at his calendar. It was spring, and a warm one at that. The ice hotel was probably nothing more than a mud puddle now. Maybe it could be a possibility for next year.

Next year? How long did he think it was going to take to bring Katie around? He thought of the stubborn look on her face when he'd invited her out on his motorcycle. He sighed. It well could be next year. He filed the ice-hotel idea in case he needed it later.

Margot came back in with something else.

"Is that what you meant?" she asked uncertainly, gesturing at the untidy stack of mismatched papers in front of him. "I wasn't quite sure what you wanted when you asked me to canvas my friends about a perfect date."

Ursula was a friend of Margot's? Good grief. His secretary had a whole secret life...that he absolutely didn't want to know about!

"Hey," he said brightly, "I wasn't quite sure myself. Just tossing out ideas. It wasn't actually for me, personally."

"I told my cousin the, um, personal item was a little over the top, but again, I didn't quite know what you were asking for."

"I thought Daredevils should try and take a hard look at how to grow our female market. I was interested in how women think. What they like. Tap into their secret romantic desires as part of a marketing scheme." He was babbling, and he let his voice drift off. "You know."

She looked, ever so faintly, skeptical. "You seem to have a pretty good grasp on what women like."

"I just needed some original ideas. I wanted to think outside the box." His box anyway, because to date, not a single item in his little box of tricks seemed to have even the remotest appeal to Katie.

"This isn't about business, is it?" Margot guessed suddenly, her eyebrow lifted, her hand on her hip.

He coughed, glowered at her, took a sudden interest in tossing a foam basketball from the dozen or so he kept on his desk through the hoop above his office door.

"I've never seen you like this," Margot said.

"Like what?" he said defensively. He missed the basket with his second effort, too. He had not missed that basket for at least three months, no matter what he had said to Margot earlier.

"I don't know. A little unsure. I hesitate to use the word *desperate* but it comes to mind. Have you met somebody special?"

"No!" he said. Despite the quickness of his reply and the empathy of it, a little smile appeared on Margot's lips. *Knowing.* His fear of being easy to read grew.

"Somebody has you rattled," she said, not without delight, when he missed the basket for the third time. It was horrible that she had stumbled on his exact turn of phrase for how Katie Pritchard was making him feel.

"That's not it at all!" he said.

"Boy, I'd like to see the girl that has you in a knot like this."

"I…am…not…in…a…knot." He said each word very slowly and deliberately. If Margot had seen what the girl who had him in a knot was wearing today she probably would have died laughing. Katie had had on some kind of horrible wrinkled smock that made her look pregnant.

But the outfit was deceptive, because it made her look like the kind of girl who should have fallen all over herself when he suggested in-line skating in the park. Instead, she had slipped her glasses down her nose and looked at him, regally astonished by the audacity of his invitation, as if she was the queen.

"I'm not dressed for skating," she'd said, just as if it wouldn't have been a blessing to wreck that dress in whatever way she could.

"It doesn't have to be today," he'd countered, registering he might be making progress. It had not been an out-and-out no.

"In-line skating," she'd said, making him hold his breath when it seemed as if she might be seriously contemplating the suggestion. But then, "No, sorry, it's not on my list of the one hundred things I have to do before I die," she'd said.

"You have a list?"

She'd gone quiet.

"Come on, Katie, give. Tell me just one thing on it."

"No."

"Why not?"

"Because it would become part of this ridiculous campaign you're on, and before I knew it I'd find myself riding an elephant in Africa."

"Is that on your list?" he asked. He couldn't have been more surprised. She didn't even want to ride a motorcycle right here in North America!

"It was just an example."

"You sure like to play your cards close to your chest." Which, since he'd mentioned it, he snuck a quick look at. Gorgeous curves, neatly disguised by the wrinkly sack she was wearing. He looked up. She was blushing. With any other girl that might mean progress, but with her you never could tell. More likely his sneaked peek had set him back a few squares. Since he had yet to get past "go," that was a depressing thought.

To offset the depression, he said, aware he was pleading, "Just tell me one thing off your hundred mustdo's. I promise I won't use it. I'll never mention it again." He gave her his Boy Scout honor look, which was practically guaranteed to win the instant trust of fifty per cent of the human race—the female fifty per cent.

She had fixed those enormous hazel eyes on him—

they had taken on a shade of gold today—and looked hard at him over the rims of her glasses. No one looked at him the way Katie did. The rest of the world saw the image: successful, driven, fun loving, daring, but it always felt as if she stripped him to his soul. The rest of the world fell for whatever he wanted them to believe he was, but not her.

Still, when she gave him that look, so intense, so stripping, the ugliness of whatever outfit she was wearing suddenly faded. It was an irony that he didn't completely understand that the uglier she dressed, the more he felt as if he could *see* her.

She shrugged. "I'd like to swim with dolphins," she admitted, but reluctantly. He was sorry he'd promised he wouldn't use it to convince her to go out with him, because he had suddenly, desperately, wanted to see her swim with dolphins.

Hopefully in a bikini, though he was startled to discover that was not his main motivation. He wanted to see her in a pool with dolphins: laughing at their silly grins, stroking their snouts, mimicking their chatter. He wanted to see her happy, uninhibited, sun kissed. Free.

Had she been that once? Before her marriage had shut something down in her? He wanted to see her like that!

Okay, the bikini would be a bonus. Though judging from what she was wearing at the moment, Katie in a bikini was a pipe dream. If she owned a bathing suit at all, it was probably akin to a bathing costume from the twenties, complete with pantaloons.

"I'm going to put that on my list, too," he'd said, amazed by how deeply he meant it.

"You promised you wouldn't do that!" she said, and

actually looked pleased because she had assumed he had broken his word so quickly.

"Not with you," he said. "I'm putting swimming with dolphins on my list to do by myself someday."

For a moment in her eyes, he saw the answer to why he was keeping at this when she wanted him to believe he would never succeed. She had *flinched*, actually hurt that he didn't want to pursue the dolphin swimming with her.

She'd snorted, though, to cover up that momentary lapse in her defenses. "You don't have a list."

"Okay, so I'm going to start one."

"And you don't do things by yourself. If you ever swim with dolphins, I bet you have a woman with you. A gorgeous one, not the least bit shy about falling out of a bikini that is three sizes too small for her."

"You're talking about Heather," he sulked. "It's over. You should know. You sent the flowers." No need to tell Katie the flowers had been dumped on the seat of his open convertible. It would probably up her estimation of Heather by a few notches.

"Dylan," she said patiently, "your women are largely interchangeable, which is why I am determined not to become one of them."

"Planet Earth calling Dylan," Margot said, giving him a bemused look.

"Sorry. I was thinking about something. But that doesn't mean I'm in a knot!"

"Of course you aren't in a knot," Margot said soothingly. "Want some advice?"

"No."

Margot ignored him. "Just be yourself."

Well, that was easier said then done because as his

sister had very rudely pointed out to him, in the past year he had become someone none of them knew. He was trying to find his way back to himself, and somehow, in a way he did not quite fully understand, Katie could help him back to that. In the same way he could help her back to the woman he sensed she once had been. But trying to get through to a woman who did not want to be gotten through to was brand-new and totally frustrating territory for him.

He waited for Margot to leave, picked up yet another letter from the pile. This wasn't half-bad. Celeste's dream date was a trip to the city, a quiet dinner, live theater, and a horse-drawn carriage ride afterward. He made a few calls. There was lots going on in Toronto, just a short drive away, but for live-theater options he narrowed it down to *The Phantom of the Opera* or a light romantic comedy called *The Prince and the Nanny.*

Both sounded equally as oppressive to him, so what girl could resist that? For a moment, Margot's voice sounded inside his head, *Just be yourself,* but he managed to quash it. He'd already tried being himself, with the motorcycle and the in-line skating offer.

No, this was much better. He'd go to her world. Not today, though. He didn't want to seem too eager or too persistent. He didn't want her to think he was a stalker, after all.

Still, the next afternoon he felt like a warrior girding his loins as he began the long walk to the business next door.

CHAPTER FOUR

THE GODS hated her. There was no other reason she was being subjected to such torture. In the last ten days Dylan had pulled out all stops. He was making it so much harder to say no to him that he no longer seemed to even notice what she was wearing! No matter how hideous the outfit—and many of them were plenty hideous—he seemed to see her. He seemed to see right through all the disguises to who she really was.

Still, despite that, it was more than evident to Katie that this had become a game to him. Dylan McKinnon was a competitor and a formidable one. He did not lose, he did not take no for an answer.

But he also took no prisoners. She knew that from a year of sending flowers for him. That fourth goodbye bouquet was as inevitable as the coming of the darkness after a day of luscious sunshine. Her effort to protect her heart from him had triggered his most competitive impulses.

She'd been invited to six different plays, all of which she wanted desperately to see. She'd been invited hiking, fishing and in-line skating. She'd been invited to dinners, sporting events, to meet celebrities. Oh, and she couldn't forget the motorcycle ride, over which she still felt a crippling regret, a swooshing sensation in her stomach, every time she thought of that glorious afternoon that had not been.

Still, the barrage was beginning to tell on her. It was getting so that she jumped every time the door to her shop opened. She was feeling like a nervous wreck, her very skin seemed to tingle, in the way that limbs that had gone numb tingled when they came back to life.

That's what was happening to her, whether she wanted it to or not. She had a feeling of being acutely, vibrantly alive.

Alive in a way she had not felt alive in a long, long time. She had not even been aware of the hibernation state she had fallen into, until he came along, woken her up, made demands of her, challenged her.

She glanced at the clock. Nearly one. She sidled over to the window. There he was, right on schedule. While she looked worse and worse—albeit deliberately—he looked better and better.

Today he was wearing jogging pants that hung low on his hips, an old Blue Jays jersey with no sleeves, a ball cap pulled low over his eyes against the brilliance of the spring day. Despite how new the days of spring were, Dylan was beginning to look sun-kissed, golden. It wasn't even possible. He had to be artificially tanning. She could never respect a man who used a tanning bed.

Was Dylan stopping?

Her traitorous heart hammered as if it couldn't care a less whether he used a tanning bed! He *was* slowing. The wild beat of her heart reminded her what it was to feel so *alive*.

She made a mad dash for the security of her counter—she was going to be in better shape than him if this kept up—and made a great show of stuffing flowers into a bouquet that she had no order for. Begonias for beware. Tuberoses for dangerous pleasures. And then her fickle fingers plucked a pink camellia—for longing—out of one of the jugs. And some gloxinia for love at first sight.

She had left her door open today, and so the bell didn't even ring warning her he was there, looking at her. She smelled him.

A scent more delicious than the aroma of spring that wafted through her door—masculine, tangy, mountain pure—and enveloped her.

"I like the way you look when you work," he decided after a long moment.

How could he possibly not notice these overalls? Any reasonable man would have seen overalls printed with huge pink peonies and vibrant green vines as a deterrent, but not him.

Peonies symbolized shame, which is what she felt about her inability to control the wild thudding of her heart as soon as he was around. They had other meanings, too. *Happy life. Happy marriage.* She had dared to dream those dreams once. She was over it.

She shoved the flower arrangement away from herself. *Don't ask.* "And how do I look when I work?"

"Intense. As if those flowers speak a language and you understand it."

"Hmm." She glanced at the bouquet. It spoke a language all right. It told her she was a woman dangerously divided.

"And also you stick your tongue out when you work."

"I do not!"

"Umm-hmm, caught right between your front teeth, like this."

She looked at his tongue. A mistake.

"I see you managed to lose the sleeves for your shirt," she said, not wanting him to notice that she was a woman who looked at a man's tongue and understood the meaning of pink camellia in a way she never quite had before.

"I ripped them off. By the way, we're completely bogged down on that jacket design. Runners *like* no sleeves."

Especially runners built like him. No sleeves. Show off those newly tanned arms. Get any girl you wanted.

Naturally that was the only reason for his persistence. No one had played hard-to-get with him before. Though she didn't feel as if she was *playing*. Running for her life was more like it. If she ran any harder, she was going to have to start looking for a sleeveless jacket of her own!

"Are you tanning?" she said, as if that was the mystery she was trying to solve by looking at his bare arms for far too long.

"Tanning? Even I haven't hit the beach yet."

"Not that kind of tanning!" *The vain kind.*

He actually threw back his head and laughed. "Katie, you have me so wrong. I'm not that kind of guy."

That's exactly what she was afraid of. That she wanted him—no, desperately needed for him—to be vain and self-centered, and that he wasn't. A part of her was always insisting it knew exactly who he was.

"Tell me you can't picture me in a tanning bed," he pleaded.

She wasn't even sure what a tanning bed involved beyond absurd self-involvement. Nudity? She could feel a blush that was going to put that pink camellia to shame moving up her neck.

"So, what can I do for you today?" she asked, all brisk professionalism.

"Say yes," he said, placing both hands and his elbows on the counter, leaning over it, fixing his gaze on her.

"You haven't asked me anything yet!" Except if she could picture him on a tanning bed, and she was not saying yes to that! Even if, despite her best efforts to stop it cold, a sneaky picture was trying to crowd into her head.

"I know, but just to surprise me, say yes."

"Is it your birthday?"

"No."

"Then I have no occasion to surprise you."

"Would you surprise me if it was my birthday?"

She was hit with an illuminating moment of self-knowledge. She was coming to love these little conversational sparring matches. She only pretended to hate them. She only pretended to herself that she wanted him to keep on running by her door. In some part of her, that she might have been just as content to keep a secret from herself, she would be devastated if he stopped popping in.

He was delivering what she needed most, even if she wanted it the least: he was delivering the unexpected; he was shaking up her comfy, safe little world; he was making her *want* again.

Dylan McKinnon was a born tease, a born charmer. He had a great sense of humor and a delightful sense of mischief. Whether she wanted to admit it or not, these spontaneous, unscheduled interchanges added spark to her day, brightness to her world, a lightness to her step. Not that she would ever let him see anything beyond her aggravation.

"No, I wouldn't surprise you even if it was your birthday. I'm not the kind of person who does surprises well."

She knew, even if he wouldn't admit it, that was the biggest surprise of all to him. That anybody could say no to him. Some days it was all that gave her strength. Knowing if she ever weakened and said yes, it would be the beginning of the end. Before she knew it she'd be getting the equivalent of the fourth bouquet—the nice-knowing-you bouquet.

"*Au contraire,* Katie, my lady, I think you are full of the most amazing surprises."

His voice had gone soft, his gaze suddenly intent, stripping. He did this—went from teasing to serious in the blink of an eye. It left her feeling off balance, unsettled. *Alive.*

"I assure you, I am not full of surprises." But hadn't she just surprised herself by acknowledging how she was coming to look forward to his visits?

He shrugged, unconvinced. "Do you want to know when my birthday is?"

He was back to playful again, and he wagged his eyebrows at her with such exaggerated hopefulness she had to bite her tongue to keep from laughing.

"If I did want to know your birth date," she said, struggling for composure, "I could find an old baseball card, I'm sure. Just think, I could find out all kinds of interesting information about you. How much you weigh, how tall you are, all your baseball stats. I could be just like all the other girls."

"No you couldn't," he said, serious again, quiet. "You could never be like the other girls, Katie."

She didn't know if that was a good thing or a bad thing, and she was not going to let him know she cared by asking!

He sighed, looked at her with aggravation, then smiled as if he'd hit a home run. "What would you think about hitting opening day at the Ice Hotel, in Quebec? Coincidentally, it coincides with my birthday. Approximately."

She scowled at him. Looked over his shoulder. Today was the first day it had been warm enough to leave her door open, spring warmth creeping in, full of promise. It was not the kind of day that normal people thought about ice hotels.

She had seen pictures of the Ice Hotel. It was magnificent: every piece of the structure, from walls, to floors, to beds, to vodka glasses carved out of ice. Seeing the ice hotel was on her list of one hundred things she wanted to do someday, right along with swimming with dolphins. How had he managed to stumble onto something from her list?

She eyed him suspiciously. He was a man driven. He probably broke into her apartment when she wasn't there and found her list.

Then she sighed. How much easier all this would be if she really could believe the worst of him. That he tanned. That he stalked. But no matter how badly she wanted to believe it to protect herself, she had that sense again, of knowing him.

She had a weird kind of trust in him even if he had spoiled the Ice Hotel for her.

Somehow, now, knowing she would be seeing it alone, when she had been invited to see it with him wrecked it for her. She would never be able to see those caribou-skin-covered beds now without wondering—

"No," she said, and her voice sounded just a teensy bit shrieky.

"Hey, it's not until next year."

"Dylan, you strike me as the man least likely to plan for something a year in advance."

"Not true. I mean, okay, I might have a slight problem with birthdays, but other than that I'm quite good at planning ahead. The next line of Daredevils jackets, for instance, will come out a year from now. If we can ever decide on a design."

"Well, the answer is still no."

"Ah," he said with a sad and insincere shake of his head, "Shot down again."

"Dylan, I wish you'd stop this."

"No, you don't," he said softly, suddenly serious again.

She folded her arms firmly over the bright pink peonies on her chest, but it didn't matter how she tried to hide those peonies. That was her shameful truth. She didn't really want this to stop, and it was nothing but embarrassing that he saw that so, so clearly.

If she really wanted it to stop, after all, she'd just say yes to something. Anything. Motorcycles or rollerblading or dinner and dancing. And then this whole thing would follow a very predictable pattern, the age-old formula for every story. It would have a beginning. A middle. And an end.

An end, as in stopped. Over. He probably wouldn't even drop in here anymore.

"I'm not going out with you, Dylan," she said. "Not ever. You must have better things to do with your time than pester me."

"Ah, Katie, my lady, oddly enough I've come to adore pestering you."

"That's what I was afraid of," she said solemnly.

He laughed. His laughter was beautiful, it twinkled through his eyes, showed the whiteness of his teeth, the strong column of his throat. He laughed from his belly, with sincere enjoyment, a contagious *joie de vivre*. But his laughter just made her more aware of how much she stood to lose the moment she said yes.

Sitting at his desk, throwing foam basketballs at his net and missing with heart-wrenching regularity, Dylan McKinnon was struck by inspiration.

He realized he had been going about this the wrong way. He'd asked Margot to find out for him what girls liked, and gotten more than what he bargained for when their answers had poured in. He'd tried to talk Katie into doing what he liked, but with the same result.

But he had always known she wasn't like any other girl he'd ever met. Her ability to say no to him being an unfortunate case in point.

It was time to tackle this differently.

He thought about what he knew about Katie for sure. He knew she was heartbroken.

Aside from that he knew she liked books and possibly cats. She was devoted to the library.

She wanted to swim with dolphins. And he knew

he'd seen just the tiniest flicker of interest in her eye when he'd mentioned the Ice Hotel.

Absently he did an Internet search. Cats + books + libraries.

Astonishingly he got a hit, and it was close to home, too. The gods had taken pity on him, seen the worthiness of his mission. Because there it was, as simple as that: the event she would find irresistible. The Toronto Public Library was hosting a fund-raising meet and greet with famous cat cartoonist Tac Revol. Tickets, naturally, were sold out, an obstacle that meant absolutely nothing to Daredevil Dylan McKinnon. By the end of the week, he had them.

He walked into her store, practically swaggering with confidence. He paused and studied her. She was trying not to acknowledge him. Could she possibly be miffed that he had not been in here every day? Oh, yes, he thought happily, that seemed to be a distinct possibility! Did she look different?

Yes, much worse than she had a week ago. She had her hair loose, which was unusual, but the style was uninspiring, lying limp to the curve of a shoulder hidden by a ruffled neckline. The skirt was a multilayered affair in several deep and distressing shades of purple.

She looked everywhere but at him. Then she met his eyes, smiled with bright phoniness, and said, "So, have you met someone new? Time to send out your famous let's-get-to-know-each-other bouquet?"

Ah, so that's why she thought he hadn't been around. "No, I haven't met anyone new," he said.

"Well, time's awasting," she said, still spilling over with phony brightness. "If you're going to keep up your same schedule, a woman a month, for this year, you'll have to get busy."

How right his sister had been. No decent girl wanted to go out with a guy like that.

"One of my clients left me her granddaughter's phone number, even though I advised her not to." Un-Katielike, she was babbling. More hurt that he had not been by than she would ever admit?

He was not even going to answer her about some-body's granddaughter. As if he would ever phone a girl he had never met. No sense telling Katie that. His sister probably would not believe him, either. A man who had turned over a new leaf had to prove it. No one was going to take his word for it. But had he turned over a new leaf? There was that feeling again, of not knowing himself.

Without a word he laid the tickets on the counter.

She glanced at them, and went to push them back. But as her hand touched them, she really looked at the tickets, and her eyes went round. He was very pleased. It was so evident she *coveted* those tickets.

"Tac Revol," she breathed. "Ohmygod. How did you get these? They're harder to come by than two scoops of pistachio on the moon!"

"I thought you might like them," he said solemnly. The look on her face had been what was harder to come by than two scoops of pistachio on the moon. He had managed, finally, to make her happy. The shadow of wariness disappeared from her features.

"For me?" she breathed with disbelief and delight. And then the unexpected happened. She picked up *both* tickets, and began to dance around her shop. She came out from behind the counter and whirled by him hugging *both* tickets to her bosom.

The dress suddenly didn't seem so monstrously ugly as the full skirt moved around her, twirled up to show a beguiling glimpse of legs so long and slender his mouth went dry. Her long hair was doing gypsy things, and the neckline of the blouse had slipped sideways, showing him the creamy perfection of her skin, the curve of her shoulder.

After he'd watched her drop that vase full of roses, and trip over the edge of a rug, he'd always kind of written her off as a klutz. But now he saw how wrong he had been.

She was graceful and sensual, at ease in her body.

But he could see the truth now, so clearly it hurt his head.

True beauty had a shine to it.

A shine that could not be disguised, or manufactured, either.

Katie Pritchard was beautiful.

He registered this fact slowly, stunned. It had been necessary for him to become a better man to even begin to see the truth about her.

Really, now was the time to break it to her that only one ticket was for her. And the other was for her escort. Him.

But somehow he didn't want to stop the dance, kill the radiant smile on her face. And somehow he needed some time alone with this astonishing revelation. Katie was beautiful. In a way that could change a man's life in ways he was not prepared to have it changed.

He thought of what he had come to know about her over the past year, and even more in the past two weeks:

that she was funny and shy and smart and sassy. And eminently decent. He realized exactly why he had avoided girls like her.

"My Mom is going to be in total shock," she told him, finally, stopping in front of him. Her brow was just a little dewy from exertion, her breath was coming in faint pants.

A shameful waste of passion.

"She has tried everything to get tickets to this event," Katie rushed on. "She even offered her first-born child. Which would be me. Oh, I could just kiss you!"

He closed his eyes and puckered up, but nothing happened. When he opened them again, she had whirled away, was in the back room on the phone. He felt an astonishing *yearning* to know what her lips would have tasted like, even though he now knew her to be far more dangerous than he had ever guessed.

Well, to his detriment, he had never shown nearly enough caution around anything dangerous.

"Mom," she said, breathlessly into the phone, "You'll never guess what just happened. I have tickets to Tac Revol!"

He stood there for a moment, letting her excited voice wash over him, thinking maybe he was too late. She already was a crazy cat lady, that was the only type of person who could get so excited about those tickets!

He was aware, suddenly, almost sadly, that he had gotten exactly what he wanted. He had transformed her. This was the moment he had waited for and worked toward. His stated mission was over, except for the going-out-with-him part.

He had *seen* her. Passionate. Laughter filled. Playful.

This moment had come out of nowhere, a gift almost as good as getting to see her swim with dolphins. But what was even more astonishing than having *seen* her was the glimpse of himself. This was the kind of girl a man could fall in love with, before he even knew what had happened.

A woman who loved her mother. He was not sure any of his other recent girlfriends had ever mentioned a mother to him!

Love. He didn't like it that that word had entered his mind in connection with Katie. Thankfully, she was the kind of girl a man like him was not really worthy of since he was not certain he could sustain this new and honorable self for long enough. He might even have bad genetics.

His father had managed a pretext of honor for thirty-five years! His father had taken a vow to love and honor and cherish, through better or worse, and he had broken that vow. He had institutionalized his wife. If that wasn't bad enough, he was reluctant to go and see her. Dylan was willing to bet it had been more than two months since his father had visited his mother. He suspected a new lady friend. And then his sister wondered what was wrong with *him* when he could not bring himself to return his father's calls? The events of his mother's illness had sent Dylan into a state of shock. He could not believe the fabric of a life that had seemed so strong, so real, could be so easily torn. He had become a man who did not believe in anything anymore.

And yet, looking at Katie talking to her own mother, he thought, *A man could believe in that.*

He realized the enormity of his error. He'd told himself he had been trying to give her back something she had lost. Now he saw he had tried to give her back what he missed about himself.

Hope. Belief. Trust.

He was not the man for this task. Foolish to have taken it on.

Katie glanced at him. Suddenly her whole demeanor changed. "Mom, I'll call you back."

"Dylan?"

"Huh?"

"Are you okay?" She came out of the back room, came and stood looking up at him.

He pasted his breeziest smile on his face, tried to see the plain Jane in her. But he saw something else. A girl who needed a man who could be one hundred per cent real. Katie needed someone brave enough to trust her with who he was once he laid down the shield.

He folded his arms over his chest. He wasn't ever having a relationship with her. He'd done the decent thing. He'd given her back her spirit, however briefly. Both of them knew now that it had only been hidden, not lost.

And what of his own spirit?

He was aware of his lack, that he had overdeveloped many sides of his personality: strength, daring, persistence. Others he had managed to totally ignore: sentiment, softness, vulnerability. If he let this thing with Katie go any further, he was going to get to the place where he really hurt, and dammit, he didn't want to go there! He was not the least bit interested in discovering his own humanity, what lay beyond the fearless facade.

He was about fun and danger, and lovely combinations of both. He was not about self-discovery. In fact he could honestly say he hated stuff like that. Nothing could bring on that nice-to-have-known-you bouquet faster than a girlfriend wanting to have a deep and meaningful conversation.

"Dylan, what's wrong?"

"Nothing," he said.

She looked doubtful. "Did you want to see Tac Revol?"

"Excuse me?" he said, lifting an eyebrow at her. "Like, I'd be caught dead at something like that!"

For a moment she looked unconvinced, and then her face relaxed.

"Oh. Of course you wouldn't! You probably don't even know Tac Revol spells Cat Lover, backward. You've just been so persistent. I thought, oh, never mind what I thought." Her smile came back. "So, you don't care if I take my mom?"

"I'm glad you're taking your mom." He ordered himself to stop talking. *McKinnon, get out. Get out with your life. Full retreat.* "I wish I could make my mom so happy. Just one more time."

"Is she gone, Dylan?" she asked softly.

Such a complicated question. "Yes," he said gruffly. She was gone. The mother of his youth, brilliant, witty, warm, loving, capable, sensitive, she was gone. And she was never coming back.

"Oh, I'm so sorry."

Everything brave and fearless in him was collapsing in the face of the light in her eyes, the wariness washed from them, replaced with something so warm, a place a man could lay down his shield and rest his head.

Katie Pritchard was beautiful in a different way than he had ever experienced beautiful before.

Hers was a kind of beauty that changed the things it

touched, made them need to be worthy of her. She was deep and real and genuine, and she'd already been stuck with one guy who wasn't anywhere near worthy of those things, who could not live up to her standard.

And that knowledge of her and what would be required of any man who linked his life with hers, even temporarily, made him feel oddly fragile, as if he had inadvertently touched something sacred. He was aware of feeling the route he was on had taken a dangerous twist and become very, very scary. Scary? But that was impossible. The Daredevil Dylan McKinnon was fearless. A little snip like her was not going to bring him to his knees.

Or maybe she was.

Because she reached up and touched his cheek with her hand, soothingly, as if she understood all the secrets he was not telling her.

And then she kissed him.

Her lips were unspeakably tender, they invited him to tell her everything, they called to the place in him that he had been so fierce about guarding, that he had revealed to no one.

It was a place of burdens and loneliness, and the burdens felt suddenly lighter, and the loneliness felt like it was fog that sun was penetrating.

"If you want to go for coffee sometime," she said, hesitantly.

He reeled back from her. "I have to go out of town for a while," he said, and saw her flinch from the obviousness of the lie.

But he felt as if it was better—far better—to hurt her now than later. The fabric of life, and especially of love, was fragile after all. He could not trust himself not to damage what he saw blossoming in the tenderness of her eyes.

Love. He could not trust himself with love.

CHAPTER FIVE

KATE took up her post beside her window, glanced at the clock. Nearly one o'clock and no Dylan. Just as there had been no Dylan for the past three days. No dropping by her shop, no teasing, no exotic invitations. Ever since she had accepted the tickets from him—and made the mistake of telling him she was available for coffee—it was as if he had dropped off the face of the earth.

The chase was over. For a guy like him it was all about the chase. She knew that from sending his flowers.

He had told her he had to go away, but she could see his red sports car parked right up the street. He certainly didn't have to let her know his schedule!

Still, this *feeling* inside her should serve as a warning. She missed him coming by. Each day she chose an uglier outfit in anticipation of it. Today she had on a pair of daisy-printed culottes and had her hair tied with a matching bandanna. It was a lot of trouble to have gone to if he wasn't going to come by and appreciate it.

For all that she had thought she was winning this game of cat and mouse they had been playing, she now realized she hadn't been at all.

She'd been kidding herself, falling more in love with

him every day. The tickets to the Tac Revol reading had finished her really, swamped her with tenderness for the man she wanted—no, needed—so desperately to hate. And when he had choked up, at the mention of his own mother, it was like the armor around her heart had been pierced irreparably.

And then he'd stopped coming, proving her instincts had been correct. Saying yes to him, inviting him for coffee, was the beginning of the end. Except her end seemed to have come without the stuff that was supposed to come in the middle. Ridiculous to feel regret.

Probably Dylan had seen something in her face that day she took the tickets that had frightened him off. *Girl who cares too much, feels too deeply, capable of sappy behavior over small gestures.*

Good, she tried to convince herself. Good that he had lost interest in his game. She had no hope of coming out the winner in any kind of match with him.

It was five minutes past one. He wasn't coming. He wasn't running today, or if he was he was avoiding her shop.

She felt her heart drop, hated it that she felt her throat close and her eyes prick as if she was going to cry! She would not cry. Her assistant, Mrs. Abercrombie, was working today. People came in all the time!

Stop it! She ordered herself. She'd known all along this was the danger of dancing with a man like that. That is what they had been doing, the last weeks, dancing, circling around each other, jousting.

A dangerous dance, because how could you spend any kind of time with a guy like that and not want more?

Not more of the good looks and charm, not more of the fun-loving playboy persona.

No, more of the other things, the more subtle qualities, the ones he tried to hide. Depth. Gentleness. Compassion. Intelligence.

More of the look in his eyes and on his face when he had said his mother was gone. She had seen who he really was then: a warrior who somehow felt he had failed, who was looking at his arsenal of weapons helplessly, not understanding how they had not worked to hold back the flow of life, to keep pain at bay from those he loved. In that moment, when he had mentioned his mother, she had seen how furiously and fiercely he loved, and she knew just why he was intent on pursuing the superficial.

And she knew just why she wanted to be the one he finally chose to lay down his weapons for, to come home to.

Her heart wanted it so badly. Her head said, pragmatically, *never going to happen.* Katie pulled her shoulders back and shoved out her chin, tucked her hair neatly behind her ears.

She was a divorced woman, not a schoolgirl. She already knew about the daggers hidden in the cloak of love. She had known all along she should not let her defenses down, and she had thought she was succeeding. Now she saw her defenses had started to come down the first day she had given in to the impulse to watch him run.

She had been realistic from the start, she had known he was not a man any intelligent woman should be pinning her hopes on. She had known all along she was a momentary distraction. She had known all along that some girl would come along who was his type—dumb, beautiful and built, a girl who allowed him to keep his fearless facade in place—and that would be the end of his interest in her.

The day was gorgeous, and she needed to focus on that—on the robin singing in the tree outside her window, in the solace of her flowers. She decided to put some buckets of flowers outside the door.

But when Katie looked at her finished display, she knew she wasn't as done thinking about him as she wanted to be. To people walking by it would only look pretty. Not a single soul but her would know what it meant. Unconsciously she had chosen larkspur, primroses, yellow lilies. She had lined her outer windowsill with little garden-ready containers of marigolds.

Dylan's worst character traits were all represented: fickleness, inconsistency, false expectations. The marigolds might have been unfair. She shouldn't really call him cruel—he had given her the Tac Revol tickets—but it did feel cruel that he had lost interest as quickly as he had gained it. That she had come to look forward to him coming by, anticipate it, *live for it,* and he had stopped.

At the last moment she added a bucket of gladiolas to her display. The flower of the gladiators, of warriors, representing strength. True strength, not just physical strength, but strength of spirit. She eyed her choice wondering if it represented her or Dylan.

Without warning, his office door flew open, and Dylan stepped out into the bright sunshine.

For a moment Katie hoped he had seen her, fantasized that he would come over and tell her what urgent matter had kept him away for the past few days.

But he didn't appear to see her at all. Slighted, she went to duck back inside her own door, but something in his demeanor stopped her. He was looking vaguely frantic, his eyes scanning the parked cars, when she could clearly see where he had parked his own car.

Dylan, frantic? She frowned. Something wrong with that picture. He never looked anything but polished—some might go as far as to say perfect—even in his jogging clothes, but he wasn't in his jogging clothes, and he looked faintly disheveled. His shirt was white and crisp, but his tie was undone, his sleeves rolled up. He had left his desk in a hurry.

None of her business, she told herself, but instead of stepping in to the relative safety of her shop, and away from any kind of engagement with him, some kind of automatic pilot took over. She stepped out, touched his arm.

He started, and that's when she realized, despite the rather gaudy outfit she was wearing for his benefit, he hadn't even seen her.

He couldn't have dismissed her that completely from his life in three short days!

"Dylan, what's wrong?"

He looked at her, and she knew she was seeing something she might never see again. Dylan was afraid.

He fumbled with his keys. "The hospital just called. Tara was brought in by ambulance."

Tara. One of his standbys. How had she managed to forget this about him when she was inviting him for coffee?

"They can't locate Sam."

"Sam?"

"My sister, Tara's, husband. They wouldn't say very much on the phone. Or maybe I didn't hear much beyond *scheduled for surgery.*"

"Tara is your sister?" she asked, flabbergasted. And then she saw the look on his face. He had his keys out, and Kate noticed his hand was shaking ever so slightly. She plucked the keys from him.

"I'll drive you. I'll just let Mrs. Abercrombie know I'm leaving."

She expected argument, at least a token protest, but there was none.

"Thanks, Katie," he said, and then he looked at her. Really looked at her, and she knew she could put out all the buckets of larkspur in the world, it wasn't going to change how she felt. The whole world could believe he was a daredevil, beyond fear, if they wanted to. In his eyes in that moment, she saw how deeply he cared for those rare people who were close to him, just as the other day she had seen how he cared about his mother. She saw that he, without hesitation, would lay down his life to protect those he cared about.

She saw, clearly, why he was so quick to get rid of women from his life.

Because he was the kind of man who, when he gave his heart, it took every single thing that he had. Caring so much was the place that weakened him, that made him afraid. No one could understand that fear of being destroyed by love as well as a woman who had lost a baby.

Katie understood she had a job to do. She unlocked the doors of his car, and they got in. She had never been in a car where she felt so low to the ground. She looked at the gear shift, tried not to let her trepidation show.

"I think the quickest way to the hospital—"

She nearly stalled the car getting it out of the parking spot. Gamely she gave it gas, and was astonished by how the amount of power sucked her back into the seat. She slammed on the brakes, adjusted the amount of gas she gave it, tried again. A car behind her honked.

"Have you ever driven a car like this?" he asked uneasily.

"A car's a car," she said grimly, trying to force it into second. The gears ground, and he winced.

"That shows what you know. Katie, pull over. I'll drive." As annoying as it was that her Good Samaritan act had been accepted for less than thirty seconds, at least his preoccupation with her driving was keeping him from being overtaken by worry about his sister.

She wanted to ask exactly what the hospital had told him about his sister, but it seemed like a wiser course just to keep his mind on her driving. And not let him behind the wheel! If she did that, she had no doubt they would be racing through the streets of Hillsboro at record-breaking speeds. He'd probably get pulled over before he got anywhere near the hospital.

"You're not safe to drive right now," she informed him, pulling into the stream of traffic on a busier road. Another horn honked.

"Sheesh, and you are? Did you know sometimes you have this holier-than-thou way of speaking that drives me crazy?"

That could be a good thing, too, right? Lots of women would like to be the ones driving Dylan

McKinnon crazy. Or just driving him. "At least no one will get hurt if we crash at this speed."

"There's that tone again. My sister will be transferred to the old folks' home before we get to the hospital."

She decided to keep with her plan to keep Dylan's mind off his worries. "Tell me about your sister. Are you the only two children?"

"Unfortunately. Tara's seven years older than me, and I would have liked a dozen other siblings to keep her busy. So she wouldn't focus so much on me. She's a menace. Meddlesome. Opinionated. I can't believe a nice guy like Sam married her."

Underneath every single word Katie heard pure love. "You adore her," she surmised.

He glared at her. "She's a pain in the butt."

"You love her madly."

"Whatever."

"You send her flowers all the time."

"Yeah, well, mostly to bug you."

"To make me think you are something you aren't," she deduced softly.

"I'm every bit as bad as you think I am, Katie. Probably worse."

"Uh-huh."

"You were very smart never to go out with me."

"Uh-huh."

"If you don't believe me, ask my sister."

"Okay."

"And quit agreeing with me, for goodness' sake!"

"Are you afraid of something, Mr. Fearless?" But she already knew. He was terrified of the very same thing she was. *Love.* He was terrified because he knew it was a force out of his control. His sister being hurt was a reminder of that. That life could best the warrior when it came to love.

He squinted narrowly at her. "I'm terrified of your driving, actually."

She was a little rusty with the standard, and after a stop at some lights her takeoff was a bit rough. The car bucked and threw Dylan's head forward.

"And whatever you're wearing. You look like you're going to an audition for the Von Trapp Family singers. What do they call those things?"

"Culottes." Ah, he was trying so hard not to let her see his heart. But she felt as if she could see it anyway.

"Good name," he muttered. "Terrifying, right up there with blood culottes."

A good thing to know about a man, that he could keep his sense of humor, even in a crisis. A good thing to know about a man—that making wisecracks was one of the defenses in the armor around his heart. They finally pulled up to the Hillsboro Hospital at the emergency door. "I'll let you go in," she said, "and I'll go find a parking spot."

"I don't want to leave my car with you."

"Too bad. Pretend it's valet service."

He looked as if he wanted to argue, but his concern for his sister got the better of him. He got out, slammed the door, raced to the hospital entrance and disappeared.

She parked the car, but way off in a back lot, not close to any other cars. If it got scratched she was going to be blamed. And then she turned the mirror and winced at what she saw. It was one thing to play the flower girl at work, for her customers, and to bug Dylan, but to go into a public building looking as if she had made an outfit out of curtains and was ready to burst into song!

She removed the scarf, ran her fingers through her hair and shook it. There was, unfortunately, not a thing she could do about the culottes, except hold her head up high, something, thankfully, that she'd had a great deal of practice at.

She went in through the sliding emergency room doors, and had to pause to let her eyes adjust from the bright light outside.

And then she looked around.

She saw Dylan, standing by a window, but he was not alone.

He was holding a baby. The breath went out of her. The baby was nestled against his chest, thumb in mouth, his other hand tracing the outline of Dylan's lips. And if she was not mistaken, Dylan kissed those little fingers, then said something that made the baby lift his head, look at him and smile.

She could see clearly they were related. The child was obviously his sister's baby, Dylan's nephew. The baby's smile showed the promise of being at least as devastating as his uncle's was. In fact, that baby could have been Dylan's son rather than his nephew, their appearance was so similar. Both had hair the color of rich, dark chocolate, amazing blue eyes. The baby, though dimpled, already had the cheekbones and the chin that were going to break hearts.

Katie was completely taken by the contrast of what she was seeing: Dylan so strong and so sure, his arm muscles flexed to hold the baby, so pudgy and powerless, so completely trusting of his uncle.

She stared at Dylan's posture. He was comfortable, relaxed, and yet two things were very evident: his deep love of the child, and the warrior protectiveness he felt toward him.

Again, she could sense how deeply this man loved when he allowed himself to. And Dylan, man least likely to ever make a serious commitment, looked as if he had been born to be a daddy.

But watching them, she suddenly felt her own heart-break as fresh and as painful as if the wound had happened yesterday.

Once upon a time this had been her dream for herself. *Exactly.*

A strong man. A baby. A little house. A swing set. More babies. A sandbox. Cookies baking. Flower beds to supply a home-based fresh-cut flower business.

Only, her dream had died, been shattered, when she had miscarried the baby. A little boy, who would have been just a year or so older than the one in Dylan's arms.

Months in a gray fog, a place of *no* feeling. No tears. No laughter. No joy. No sense of having anything to look forward to. Marcus growing impatient, then distant. More distant than he had been before.

As the memories swamped Katie, she watched a nurse approach Dylan, tiny, perky, all smiles and bubbliness.

The kind of girl Dylan always went for—except that, as a nurse, she was probably smart.

Katie wanted to leave. Her heart hurt in ways she had not thought it could hurt.

This was the hurt she always had known Dylan was capable of inflicting. This was the hurt three days of not seeing him had begun to prepare her for. It was the hurt of a woman who wanted something terribly badly—underscored by the picture he made holding that baby—and it was like wanting two scoops of pistachio on the moon. Not just unrealistic. Impossible. Non-existent.

She drew in a deep breath, and marched up to him, just as the nurse moved away. "Here are your keys," she said brightly. "I'm going to go. I hope your sister is all right."

"She fell over some toys on the stairs," he said, but he was watching her, carefully. He made no move to take the keys. "Her leg is broken, badly. An orthopedic surgeon is on the way."

"On the way!" she said. "That's great. Well, I must—"

He took a step in to her. "What's the matter?" he asked softly.

The baby was reaching for her hair. He smelled sweet, of talcum and baby soap, and of innocence and hope and dreams.

She couldn't even do the baby bouquets at work. She let Mrs. Abercrombie fill the little blue ceramic boots and the pink stork baskets.

"The matter?" She stepped back from the baby. If he touched her with those little pudgy hands she knew she would shatter into a million pieces, and there would be no putting her back together again. "Nothing."

But her voice wobbled shamefully. She pressed the keys into his hand. "I have to—"

"Katie," he said, his voice gravelly, firm, strong, "Talk to me."

No.

A terrible thing happened. She began to cry. It felt as

if every one of those feelings she'd bottled up after the miscarriage had decided to pick this moment, of all moments, not be dammed one second longer.

It was exactly the kind of demonstration that could absolutely be counted on to horrify a man like Dylan McKinnon.

Only it didn't.

He drew her into him with his free arm, pressed her head against his chest. "Hey," he said, "Hey, it's okay."

The baby was too close now. Touching her, squawking at her like a little bird, tangling his fists in her hair.

She waited to break, to shatter, for her heart to burst into a million pieces.

Standing there with Dylan's arm around her, held fast by his strength, with the sweet-scented baby pulling at her hair and chirping away at her in baby talk, something did shatter. The ice around her heart. Only, behind it was not destruction but warmth. The loveliest warmth burst through her.

She wiped her tears on Dylan's chest, took a step back. "Can I hold him?" she whispered.

The baby came to her so willingly, gurgling and blowing spit bubbles. Her arms closed around him, and she felt his wriggling, beautiful strength.

She felt *life*. In all its mystery and all its magnificence.

She met Dylan's eyes and heard herself saying, her voice brave, "I had a miscarriage. I lost my baby. The marriage didn't make it."

He just looked at her. He didn't try and make it better, but he didn't try and look away, either. He didn't try and change the subject. He didn't offer words that would not and could not help. He just looked at her, and there was something in the look in his eyes that she could hang on to.

"Come on," he finally said. "Let's sit down over here." He guided her to the waiting room, which was blessedly empty, and she took a chair, the baby nestled happily against her. Dylan took the chair beside her, covered her hand with his own.

"What's his name?" she asked.

"Jake."

"I was going to call my baby Jonathon. It was a boy, too."

"Jonathon's a nice name. I think you would have been a good mom. No. A great one." He did not say she was young and there would be more babies, more chances, as if one child could be replaced with another.

"I took it really hard," she told him.

"Would there be any other way to take it?" he asked softly.

"Marcus, my husband, seemed relieved." She had never said that to another living soul before. Had she even said it to herself? The words were tumbling out now.

"He said 'I'm not sure I was ready for a baby.' He hadn't wanted to try again. What he'd wanted was for me to get over it. He didn't understand how you could grieve for something that had never breathed." She paused, and said so softly maybe she just said it to herself, "But my dreams breathed."

Dylan swore under his breath. One word. Not a word anyone else had said, except maybe her in the darkness of night when she had found herself so alone with a heart full of misery.

And Dylan meant it. And she knew he was a man

who would never be relieved if something happened to his unborn baby. Never.

The yearning leaped in her, clawed at her, told her, *Take a chance on him.*

On him? That was craziness! She had looked after his flowers. She knew better. Except what she had seen in his eyes just now was like a beacon that called the ships lost at sea home to safe harbor.

"If Tara's your sister," she asked, suddenly, "who's Sarah?"

He slid her a look, smiled crookedly. "PR manager."

"Margot?"

"Receptionist at my office."

"Janet?"

He sighed. "It's Sister Janet."

"I think," she decided out loud, "I'll move to another country." Was it even possible to outdistance what was unfolding within her? How far would she have to run to escape the *hope* that was unfurling inside of her?

"Katie, my lady," he said, "Oh, Katie, my lady."

Katie, my lady. Just a teasing phrase, not something that was intended to increase the yearning within her. But spoken with such tenderness, from his heart, that's exactly what it did. And it made her decide she wasn't going anywhere. Not just yet.

And then he took his hand in hers, and he kissed the top of it, and sighed, a man who would rewrite the past for her if he could.

But what would he write on her future?

The baby, who had been slurping contentedly, suddenly popped his thumb from his mouth and roared, "JAAAKE."

She laughed, startled and delighted.

"We're working on volume control," Dylan said affectionately. "He only has one setting, loud. And if I put him on the ground, he only has one speed."

"Let me guess. Fast."

"How did you guess?"

"Um. I can tell this is one acorn that didn't fall too far from the McKinnon family tree."

"Mr. McKinnon?" a nurse called. "Can you come with me for a minute?"

Dylan studied Katie. "Do you want me to leave Jake with you or take him with me?"

Katie struggled to keep her face composed. Yearning, sweet and tantalizing, burned through her. What she wanted to do was bury her face in the sweetness of that baby's scent and never come up for air again.

"Leave him with me," she whispered.

"Hey, stinker," Dylan warned his nephew sternly, "don't live up to your reputation." And then he turned and followed the nurse down the hallway.

Katie watched him go, and even though she knew better, even though she was trying so hard not to get any more entangled with a man who could exercise so much power over her—without any awareness of that power on his part—she felt her treacherous heart go right down the hall with him.

Dylan found his sister. She was being prepped for surgery and needed to give him some instructions, but he was having trouble focusing on her completely.

He wanted to kill somebody, or at least hurt them badly. He wanted to kill a man he'd never met before. He wanted to kill the man who had been so self-centered he'd left Katie all alone with her grief for that unborn child. What had she said? Her husband had been *relieved.*

Dylan couldn't believe a man could look into those eyes and not find it in himself to be there, one hundred per cent for her. Not *want* to be there for her.

"No chocolate, candy, choking-size hazards, hamburgers or steak and lobster," his sister said.

Dylan focused on Tara. Sheesh. She had been given something to control pain until her surgery. "What are you talking about?" he asked her.

She sighed elaborately. "Earth calling Dylan. I'm trying to tell you how to take care of a baby."

"Me?" he said. Katie's face faded from his mind and he focused on his sister. "I'm not looking after Jake. Where's Sam?"

"San Francisco. Fogged in. So unless you want your favorite nephew to go to foster care, time to step up to the plate." She giggled helplessly. "Step up to the plate. Get it? That's priceless, given your old career."

"Ha, ha," he said without an ounce of humor. "When's Sam going to get in?"

"Dylan, I have no gift for predicting the weather even when I'm not on drugs."

After getting a ton more of unhelpful advice from his sister, Dylan went back down the hall to the emergency waiting room. Katie had found a box of toys, and was now sitting on the floor with his nephew, unmindful of getting her outfit dirty; though of course that was, one would assume, why you wore an outfit like that. You wouldn't worry about wrecking it, you'd hope you could! Thank goodness, she had lost the babushka somewhere.

Or maybe not. Because without it, her hair fell like a shining wave to the slenderness of her shoulder.

As always happened, it felt as if it was not the outfit he saw at all. It was the look on her face, the sweet curve of her smile.

He realized why he had been so anxious to focus on the killing of her ex-husband. Because to focus on her was to threaten what remained of his tattered control after he had seen her do her spontaneous little dance over the Tac Revol tickets, after he had tasted the clearbrook sweetness of her kiss.

There was a look on her face as she studied Jake that was rapt, even more beautiful than when she had danced. She looked serene, almost like a Madonna.

A decent girl. A wholesome girl. A smart girl. *A girl absolutely born to be a mother.*

He was well aware that there on the cold hospital floor sat a woman he'd offered everything to: he'd offered to wine and dine her, escort her to the most-sought-after functions, take her on his motorcycle, give her dreams carved in ice.

She'd said no to each of his invitations without even a moment's hesitation. And then when he'd finally done something genuinely nice—as accidental as it may have been that she thought those tickets were for her mother—then it had been her turn to issue the invitation.

That was what Katie was doing even now, sitting on the floor, playing with the baby, shining with an inner light that was nearly blinding. She was issuing him an invitation to a life he had turned his back on when his mother had gotten ill. A life that he had decided was too full of foibles, too unpredictable, that extracted too great a cost.

That's why he had avoided her ever since she had ever so tentatively extended her invitation for coffee.

He was not unaware of a feeling of the universe conspiring against him. He'd decided, after seeing her dance with the Tac Revol tickets, after her kissing him, that the game was up. Over. The stakes had become a little too high for his tastes. And yet here he was, tangled with her again.

"Thanks, Katie," he said, coming up to her.

"Is your sister okay?"

"Whacked out on drugs. She seems to think I'd be a good candidate to look after Jake."

"Aren't you?"

What had he ever done to deserve the look of trust on her face?

"No."

"Haven't you ever looked after Jake before?"

"I've taken him out a couple of times by myself. To the mall. And the park. The little devil is a chick magnet. And the man-with-baby thing is unbelievable. The women are all over me when I have Jake." He knew exactly what he was trying to do. Put back the barrier that had been so conveniently provided by names of women she didn't know. Tara. Sarah. Janet. Margot.

"Trust you to see a baby as useful for that reason!"

"His usefulness is limited," Dylan said. It was working. She looked justifiably horrified. Part of him was thinking, *Katie, my lady, please see me in a bad light. You make the decision to not have anything to do with me. Because I can't seem to follow through when I make that decision about you.*

"The baby's usefulness is limited?" she asked, indignant.

"Oh, sure, he's cute, but he's basically a poop machine. Just when things have the potential to get interesting, he fills his pants. He actually leaked on me once. I thought I was going to hurl."

"Daredevil Dylan McKinnon was going to throw up over a little baby leak?" She started to laugh.

"Don't be so damned sanctimonious. You weren't there. The horror was unimaginable, even for someone like you, who probably has a fairly good imagination. Have you ever had to deal with a situation like that?"

"I used to babysit in high school. I wouldn't let a baby leak scare me!"

He snorted. "That's like a soldier who has never been in a combat zone saying bullets don't scare him."

"It's not quite the same thing," she said dryly.

"Yeah, well, baby leaks scare me, and I'm man enough to admit it."

"I appreciate your vulnerability," she said, tongue-in-cheek.

"Don't tell anybody. I'd be ruined. And don't you start smiling!"

Really, her smile was becoming the hardest thing to handle. It lit something in her. Had he known, right from the beginning, in some place he'd been afraid to go within himself, that her smile would be like this? *Worth it. Worth everything. Even the uncertainty of his own soul. Even coming face-to-face with all his own fears.*

"Why does everyone think me being tortured is funny?" he asked. He was asking the universe as much as her!

"Oh, Dylan, it's not exactly you being tortured that's funny. It's you being terrified of something so darling as a little baby."

That showed what she knew! "You won't think he's such a little darling when his forehead wrinkles up, he holds his breath and starts turning red."

He could see way too clearly that he was playing with something far too big now, something he might not be able to control. He'd never be able to forget the beauty he discovered, all her hopes and dreams in her face.

Wasn't that at the heart of this whole thing? Some instinct had told him she was beautiful, and he had wanted her to look beautiful again, had wanted to see those hopes and dreams shining in her face, had *needed* to know that some precious part of her had not been destroyed by whatever she had been through.

Proof his plan was working—there she sat on the floor in her Maria Von Trapp outfit, playing with baby toys, radiating absolute and extremely worrisome beauty.

"Hey," she said, looking up at him, wrinkling her nose. "Don't look so worried."

He had that sensation, watching her play building blocks with his nephew, that Katie could know him in ways he had never allowed people to know him. No one in the world ever guessed when he was feeling pressure, when he was rattled, when he was scared. Not even when he'd been posed at the door of that airplane waiting to jump had he betrayed how truly frightened he was. He'd made some wisecrack remark that had made everyone laugh.

But if she had been there he had the uneasy feeling she would have known, just as she had known to take those car keys from his hand a half an hour ago.

And Dylan McKinnon wasn't quite sure if it felt good or bad to be quite so transparent to another human being.

"So, what's the battle plan?" she asked him, brushing off her skirt/short fashion disaster and getting to her feet.

"The same as any battle plan," he told her. "Survival." And he was not sure he was referring to looking after a baby, either!

She looked askance at him. "Battle plans aren't about survival," she pointed out. "They're about victory. Winning."

Now, if anyone should know that, it should be him. He did know that. He'd had a battle plan all along, prove a decent girl would go out with him, give her the gift of hope in return and then, mission accomplished, withdraw. Now his battle plan was wavering before him like a mirage of an oasis on a blistering desert afternoon.

But now he saw it differently. Survival. His.

"I can take it from here," he said bravely. "I'll take him over to my sister's. I have her key. The place is babyproofed and supplied."

Something flitted across her face. Relief? But it was quickly replaced by another look. Determination. "You don't think I'm leaving you alone with this baby, do you?"

"I can manage a baby."

She rolled her eyes. "No, you can't."

He should have felt insulted, but he didn't. He felt relieved. And, oddly enough, not relieved at the very same time. As confused as he had ever felt. Before, even if she had been saying no, he'd felt as if he was in control. Now he didn't. And he was pretty sure Dylan McKinnon out of control was not going to be a good thing.

"Really," he said, a bit more forcefully, "I can manage it. I make million-dollar decisions every day. Forty-two people work for me. I'm the honorary spokesperson for three different charitable organizations. What is one twenty-pound baby in comparison to all that?"

She looked entirely unimpressed. "Dylan McKinnon, have you ever kept a plant alive for more than three weeks?"

"What kind of plant?" he hedged.

"Any kind. A garden flower? A houseplant?"

Mental pictures of a sordid history that included many dead, dead plants formed in his mind's eye.

"Anything *green?*" she asked, as if she was relaxing her standards to give him a chance.

"Bath towels?"

She shook her head. "Living green."

He lived in a condo. He didn't even have to remember to water the lawn! "The fact that plants, er, fail to thrive around me is irrelevant."

"Hmm. How about a puppy? Or a kitten?" She looked at him, shook her head. "A goldfish? Guppies?"

He scowled at her. "My lifestyle has never allowed for pets."

"Precisely my point. You don't know how to care for things."

"I travel! I know how to care for things! My car is cared for! That's diamond finish on the wax job in case you didn't notice."

"Living things," she amended.

Her chin was getting a stubborn set to it. A smart man would have been running. But he was in charge of a baby now, and it was hard to run with twenty pounds of squirming baby under your arm, and plus, he was thinking he kind of liked her chin pointed at him like that.

"Speaking of cars," she said, "do you have a car seat?"

And that clinched it. Dylan McKinnon knew, that whether he wanted to or not, he needed Katie Pritchard right now. Only a girl like her could be trusted to think of something as all important to his nephew's well-being as a car seat.

The baby did that wrinkly thing with his forehead, held his breath and started to turn a very unbecoming shade of red.

How humiliating. Dylan didn't just need Katie. He needed her *desperately*.

CHAPTER SIX

KATIE stared at Dylan with absolute astonishment. Here was a man who had jumped out of airplanes, bungee jumped, raced motorcycles. Here was a man who, as he had just pointed out, made million-dollar decisions, was responsible for employees, ran a company.

And yet there was an unmistakable bead of sweat on his forehead as he gazed at his nephew. His gorgeous blue eyes had a glint of pure fear in them. He was drumming his fingers nervously against the muscle of his thigh.

And all because his adorable nephew had stopped all activity—building block suddenly frozen in midair—a look of fierce concentration on his now reddening chubby face.

"Is he," Katie asked, uncertainly, "you know?"

But Dylan didn't have to answer. They were enveloped in a stench that seemed as if it could not possibly have been produced by the adorable little cherub in front of them. The look of concentration evaporated from Jake's face, he gurgled with what would seem to be self-satisfaction and returned to his blocks.

"Now what?" the president and CEO of Daredevils asked her in an undertone.

"I don't have a clue," she said.

She recognized how absurd this was. It was a baby. And it had two full-grown adults almost completely tied up in knots.

She couldn't help it. She started to laugh. When Dylan glared at her, mistakenly thinking she was laughing at his weakness instead of her own, she laughed harder. Finally, her howls of laughter petered down to sputters. She hoped she wouldn't snort. Of course she snorted.

Dylan was looking at her intently, as if he had never seen her before. More absurdity: she might have dreamed such a look over wine and dinner, with her hair upswept, diamonds sparkling at her ears, lips painted a beguiling shade of red. Such a look should be reserved for a woman wearing the perfect little black dress. But over baby poop? In hideous daisy-printed culottes? Right after she had snorted? *Welcome to your life, Katie Pritchard.* She licked her lips uncomfortably.

"You should do that more often," he decided, then looked away, as if he had said too much, revealed too much.

"What should I do more often?" she breathed, feeling her stomach drop out at the way his eyes had fastened, with searing heat, on her mouth. She might have dreamed such a look to be appropriate right before a man leaned forward to take his true love's lips with his own.

"Laugh."

Part of her had hoped he meant lick her lips!

"Okay, Mr. Daredevil," she said, "I'm waiting for the plan."

"You're the one who knows how to keep plants alive!"

A nurse came by, gray haired, very efficient looking. "If you check at the reception desk before you leave, we can lend you a car seat to take the baby home."

Dylan turned up the full wattage of his smile. Katie guessed he was going to put his charm to good use and get that diaper looked after for them.

Instead he surprised her by saying to the nurse, "Uh, we have two rank amateurs here who don't know the first thing about a messy diaper. Or maybe I should say two messy amateurs who don't know anything about a rank diaper. Could you find somebody to give us a quick lesson, before we take him home?"

The nurse smiled at him. Was nobody immune to this man's charms? " I'd be happy to show you how to change a diaper."

A few minutes later they were in a little room, the nurse not as charmed by Dylan as Katie had thought. She made him change the diaper!

Katie was not unaware, as she watched, that this was something she had thought she would be doing with her husband one day. She had looked forward to every little thing about that baby coming. Foolishly, the day she had found out she was pregnant, she had even begun to buy diapers, pajamas with feet in them, soothers, stuffed crib toys.

Now, in a room with *reality,* she wondered if Marcus ever would have tackled a mess like that! She had not allowed herself to think much about *what if.* But now she did wonder. What if they had stayed together? Would she have felt as alone with parenting as she had started to feel in their marriage?

Certainly, she could not imagine Marcus bending

over such an arduous task with such a look of grim determination on his face.

Dylan shot a look at her. "I don't have anything on me, do I?" he whispered.

"Such as?" she whispered back.

He glared at her, then at the baby. "Such as *brown*."

"You look like you're okay. So far."

The baby gurgled happily and wagged his legs.

"I wish he wouldn't do that," Dylan said grimly.

"Me, too," she admitted.

They both laughed, and the nurse joined in. The impromptu diaper changing class was a strangely intimate moment. A mommy-and-daddy kind of moment that made Katie feel that stab of longing for the life she did not have, a life that had been snatched from her by a cruel twist of fate.

That's what she needed to remember as she was admiring the confidence with which Dylan was taking on this task. She need to remind herself that life had cruel twists and turns that she had no hope of controlling. That she had withdrawn from the race for a *reason*. It could hurt too much to run.

But standing in this little room, almost shoulder to shoulder with Dylan, the pain of *not* running the race could compete with the pain of running with all your heart.

"Just hold his feet in one hand, lift him up and swab," the nurse suggested helpfully.

For a man who had made his living being a professional athlete, Dylan suddenly seemed hopelessly uncoordinated. But determined. "You take his feet," he told Katie. A small thing, but it somehow solidified them as a team.

Gingerly she did. Jake tried to kick free.

Dylan scowled at the baby as if he were a puzzle that needed to be solved, then took a deep breath and did what needed to be done.

That, Katie thought, was the kind of man he was. He wanted people to believe it was all fun and frolic about him, but that was not the truth at all. She felt as if she could see the truth about Dylan.

"You don't shirk from the hard stuff do you?" she said. That was why he was such a success at business

Dylan cast a glance at her.

"You just dig in and get the job done."

"I don't think *dig in* is exactly what I want to hear right now," he said lightly, but rather than looking pleased at her assessment, Dylan looked pensive. "That's not what my sister would tell you," he said. "She thinks I shirk from the hard stuff."

"Like what?" Katie asked, incredulous.

But he was engrossed in his task, and didn't answer. Several wrecked diapers later—the tabs would not stick once his hands were slippery with baby oil and powder—the job was done. Dylan, unaware he was dusted from head to toe with baby powder himself, looked very pleased as he lifted his nephew off the table.

"Next time, your turn."

But it seemed to her maybe next time wasn't such a good idea. She was looking for excuses to hang on to him, to hang on to the intimacy of this little mommy-daddy experience.

But really, if he could change a diaper, he was good to go.

Without her.

"My sister says that it's different when it's your own baby," he said with an easy grin. "Not so nauseating."

Your own baby.

"Are you planning your own baby?" she asked him. She said it ever so casually. Just conversation. Pathetic that she was holding her breath waiting for his answer.

"I thought that's what I wanted once, but," he suddenly looked uncomfortable, "lately I don't seem to know what I want."

There. His answer.

And yet, even though it was not what she wanted to hear, Katie appreciated Dylan was giving her something that he rarely gave. He presented himself to the world as an extremely confident man. A man who jumped out of airplanes, no hesitation. A daredevil.

And so, his showing her his doubt was a gift.

Seeing him with his nephew had brought her yearnings sharply to the surface, and sharply into focus. It had made her contemplate entering the race all over again, like a person drawn to the mystery of Everest, Mountain of Tragedy.

He didn't know what he wanted. And she felt shadows of doubt on what she wanted. A month ago her flower shop, her quiet life had been enough. Now it wasn't.

Like lightning, fear struck her. What if she lost another baby? Could she survive that kind of loss again?

Was it completely delusional to think being with a man like him would somehow make the burden of that loss a shared one?

She recognized the insanity of her own thoughts. She had never even had a cup of coffee with this man.

Really, she knew less about him than what was printed on the back of his baseball cards. And here she was weaving a fantasy that he was at the center of! *Her own baby. A home to call her own. A man like this one.*

This was precisely why she had immersed herself in her business. This was why she had made a simple life for herself: reading, her cats, taking her mother on outings. This was precisely why she had done a voluntary exit from the whole man/woman game. She wasn't strong enough to play again, to run the race again. Not yet, and maybe not ever. She reminded herself she *liked* her safe, predictable world.

Or had liked it. But maybe a small dissatisfaction had been stirring from the very moment she had given in to the temptation to watch a glorious man run.

She made the mistake of looking at the baby and his uncle.

Jake was nestled into Dylan's chest, sucking sleepily on his thumb. The picture they made caused her heart to ache. Dylan's strength and self-assurance in stark contrast to the baby's helplessness and need. Dylan was all hard lines and taut muscle, a warrior, the baby was like a little puddle of warmth and softness, the one the warrior was sworn to protect.

And yet the tenderness that glowed in Dylan's eyes when he looked at his nephew, that softened the masculine assuredness of his face, made him seem more attractive to Katie than he ever had.

And he had always seemed plenty attractive!

All her weeks of successfully resisting Dylan McKinnon were going straight down the tubes. Worse, at the moment she was feeling raw and vulnerable after the strange intimacy of the encounter in the bathroom, her confessions, his reassurances.

Katie recognized she was doing exactly what Dylan expected every single woman to do around him. She was capitulating to his charms!

It had to stop. There had to be one woman in the world who would not throw herself at his feet, and it had to be her!

And yet here she was, so taken with him she felt weak-kneed and dry-mouthed, and like she wanted to spend the rest of her life contemplating the sensual fullness of his bottom lip! Here she was, practically floating, feeling a strange and glorious little fire in her bosom because of the way Dylan's eyes rested on her, for just a touch too long, when he looked over his nephew's head.

Katie needed to remember that charm came as naturally to him as hunting came to the lion. And his charm probably fell in the same category—self-serving and predatory.

The thing to do before she was any more helplessly overwhelmed by his attractiveness, his playfulness, his allure, would be, obviously, to remove herself from this situation.

She knew she had to do it without it *seeming* as if she had to get away from him. There was nothing that would trigger a predator's instincts like prey in full flight!

A nurse came and set down a car seat beside them.

"Dylan," Katie said firmly "you take the baby home. I'll grab a cab."

Dylan glanced from her to the baby. Then back at her. That adorable doubt was playing across his normally self-assured features. "I thought I couldn't even be trusted with a houseplant," he reminded her.

"Well, you can't. But help is a phone call away, if you need it."

"Yeah," he muttered, "911." He juggled the baby and picked up the car seat.

"Here. I'll take one of those as far as your car."

"Thanks." He handed her Jake. She was glad. One more small chance to hold his warm little body, to smell the baby shampoo in his hair, to fill her senses with him.

Before she let go.

They crossed the parking lot, and she watched as Dylan struggled to fit the car seat into his nearly non-existent back seat.

"Okay," she said, "ready." Ready to let go. Ready to go back to her old life. Ready to forget the smell of babies and the look in a man's eyes.

Liar. Out loud she said, "You can call from your sister's if you need anything else from me."

There. Didn't she sound cool and composed, totally collected? She felt she had very successfully disguised the fact that she was a woman who could be wooed into a helpless, spineless jellyfish by a man with a baby in his arms!

Dylan reached for the baby. Jake whimpered.

"Come on, little man, you're coming with your favorite unkie." Dylan glared at Katie. "Don't ever tell a single soul about that."

"What?"

"Unkie," he whispered.

She juggled the baby, held up her two fingers, Scout's honor style.

"Come on, Jake," Dylan said.

The baby nestled in tight against her, sidled a look at his uncle. "NO!"

She tried to help by detaching him from her, but as Dylan reached around his tummy to take him, she found a chunky hand wrapped in her hair. Dylan's hand was brushing her breast. She felt the burn of it. Her eyes met his. He jerked his hand away.

"*NO YOU,*" the baby informed him, taking a tighter wrap on her hair. "*SHE.*"

"Jake," he said firmly, CEO of a million-dollar company, "You are coming with me. Let go."

"*NO, NO, NO,*" little Jakie shrieked. A passerby gave them a curious look.

"Shhh, little man," Dylan said. His voice, roughened with tenderness, sent shivers of new appreciation up and down Katie's spine.

The baby, however, was unimpressed. He wrapped his free arm around her neck. When Dylan reached for him again, he loosed it just long enough to slug his unkie in the ear.

"Hey, Jakie, calm down." Dylan enveloped the small fist in the strength of his own hand, and she felt another shiver of raw appreciation at how gently he leashed his strength to control the baby.

However, Jake could give her a lesson or two in being immune to the charm of Dylan McKinnon. The baby shrieked and pulled his solid little body in even closer to her. When Dylan tried one more time to pull him away, the baby busted him one in the chops.

"Here," Katie said, her maternal instincts feeling

nothing but sympathy for the poor distraught baby. "Give it up before you get seriously hurt."

"If he's going to hurt anyone it's going to be me," Dylan said with such furious protectiveness *of her* that her tummy did the roller-coaster ride down to the bottom of her stomach.

"Just see if he'll calm down."

Reluctantly Dylan moved back a step. The baby eyed him warily. Then he went limp, his fight over. Jake gave his uncle a baleful glare and settled himself against Katie's chest. After a moment, he put one thumb back in his mouth, but kept the chubby fingers of his other hand curled possessively through her hair and closed his eyes. He hiccupped sadly.

"And you've never even snuck him chocolate or taken him to the park!" Dylan said wryly. And then with satisfaction, "He's getting drool on your shirt."

"A little drool never hurt—"

But Dylan had lifted the hem of his own shirt, reached up with it, giving her a glimpse of a belly so hard and muscled her fingers actually tingled from wanting to touch. He wiped Jake's face and let the hem of his shirt drop back down.

Dangerous thoughts crowded her mind, at least partially triggered by that glimpse of Dylan's gorgeous flat belly, the very kind of thoughts she had been trying so desperately to get away from. What if this could be her real life? Her real man? Babies and baby seats, and glimpses of things that made your heart race on an ordinary afternoon. It might even be worth the diaper part.

While she was living dangerously, she stole another look at Dylan's lips, allowed herself to remember what they tasted like, allowed herself to think of the secret and sacred things that occurred between a man and a woman to make a baby.

"You try and put him in the seat," Dylan whispered.

She was dreadfully reluctant to give up the baby, but she knew this was a dangerous game she was playing. She untangled his chubby fist from her hair.

The baby's eyes popped open, he eyed his uncle with grave suspicion.

"Hey, great imitation of Chucky."

"Who?"

"Chucky. A demented doll that comes to life. Horror movie. It goes without saying that you wouldn't like it."

"Did you like it?" she asked. Surely a full-grown man wouldn't like such nonsense? A feeble excuse to find him flawed, but she was a desperate woman.

"Of course I liked Chucky. It's a classic!" He noticed the baby was relaxed, and he reached for him.

But when Dylan touched him, Jake screamed. Dylan jerked back his hand as if he'd been burned, Jake became silent. Dylan's lips twitched. He reached out. This time he didn't even have to touch the baby. Jake screamed long and loud.

Katie tucked the baby's head in close. "How do you *expect* him to behave toward someone who liked Chucky? And just for your information *Jane Eyre* is a classic."

"He doesn't know the difference between Chuck and Jane. He's not even two!"

"Babies are sensitive to vibes," she said, and as if to confirm it the baby blew some indignant spit bubbles his uncle's way and regarded him with silent challenge.

"The little devil," Dylan muttered. "He's playing a game with me. What's worse, he's winning!"

It was a rather funny thing to see one of the world's most competitive men losing a battle of will with a baby!

Finally Dylan shoved his hands in his pockets and glared at his nephew. "I've never done anything to him, honest!"

He regarded Katie and the baby thoughtfully, then grinned. "Oh, I get it. Vibes aside, you're nice and soft in all the right places."

As if to confirm, the baby snuggled deeper against her breast.

It occurred to her that Dylan was now studying her chest with grave interest. She began to blush, and then was astounded when he did, too!

Dylan backed away from her hurriedly. Katie managed to get the baby's uncooperative limbs into his car seat. Jake contemplated this development suspiciously, and Katie wondered how well Dylan was going to drive when his nephew figured out they were leaving *SHE* behind.

"Katie, hop in. Just for a few minutes. I know how the male mind works. Easily distracted. Our first stop will be Bill's Wild Toy Store. I'll get Jakie one of those windup buffalos they advertise on TV, and then, Katie, we can release you to your flower store."

Step into the car, or let him handle it himself? This was not her life, not her man, not her baby. This was not a man she would ever be making babies with. This was a man who had just given her fair warning how his mind worked.

How the male mind worked. They were a breed easily distracted. Everyone could be replaced with something or someone more entertaining, more interesting.

Even knowing that, she got in the car. She told herself it was just for Jakie's sake, not because she was reluctant to say goodbye to the little adventure life had dropped in her lap.

At Bill's Wild Toy Store, the funniest thing happened. Once inside the building, arguably every child's fantasy, Jake clung to her more tenaciously than ever. He was not trading up: he could not be wooed away from her with a three-foot-tall ride-on buffalo, foam footballs, red wagons or beach balls. Jake's lack of enthusiasm did not prevent Dylan from loading two shopping carts full of toys, one which he shoved ahead of him, and one which he dragged behind to the checkout.

How could you spend an hour shopping for toys with Dylan and keep your guard up? How could you watch him put on a passable juggling act with beanie babies and not come a whole lot closer to being in love with him? How could you watch him crashing remote control cars into the doll display with fiendish enthusiasm and not forgive him his easily distracted male mind?

The 50-per-cent-off, spring-fling sale was in full swing, and the famous toy store was full of women. Young women, old women, mom women, single women, pretty women, plain women.

To Katie, every single one of them seemed to slide Dylan the most appreciative of glances, and he seemed way more distracted by the toys than by any of those glances. He didn't even seem to notice that he was on the receiving end of rapt gazes, some that were shy, some that were openly inviting.

Some of those women looked at him as if he were a piece of art, to be admired but not touched, others let the heat of their thoughts right into their eyes, the sudden sway of their hips. It reminded her that he was the playboy and she was the plain Jane. That she was allowing herself to be sucked into a fantasy, to entertain the illusion that she and Dylan and Jake were just an ordinary little family, out shopping for toys.

For a man who had claimed to be easily distracted, he didn't even seem notice the female kafuffle he was generating. He seemed seriously and sincerely engrossed in trying out the remote-control helicopter, punching the bounce-back rubber clown, tossing the foam basketballs through the hoop that had been set up. At the basketball hoops, she was almost certain he was showing off for *her.*

She was overtaken by a feeling of *wanting* to let her guard down and just give in to liking him, enjoying him, feeling compatible with him. Within moments he had her laughing, and feeling light inside. She had seen his most secret side. She had seen the side of him that tempered his phenomenal strength with equally phenomenal tenderness, she had seen the part of him that was patient, she had seen the part that was laughter filled and joyous.

Back in the car now stuffed with their purchases, Dylan contemplated his nephew's indifference to the toys, and the new sumo wrestler hold he had on Katie.

"SHE," Jake announced, as she strapped him into the car seat. He watched the two adults on the curb.

"He's getting ready to throw himself into a prize-winning tantrum if you leave," Dylan deduced.

"You're going to have to deal with that sooner or later," she said firmly, though she didn't think in his car, dealing with the steadily building rush hour traffic, would be a good place for him to do it.

"A puppy!" Dylan announced with a snap of his fingers. "I'll get him a puppy. And then drive you back to work."

"Dylan, we have already established the fact that you cannot even be trusted with a plant. A puppy?"

"I'll bet once he has a puppy he won't even notice you're gone."

And would Dylan notice she was gone once *he* had a puppy to engage himself? Probably not.

She slid him a look. Was he trying to get rid of her? Did he sense, as she did, something deepening around them, a force gathering, beckoning, whispering?

Follow me. Come.

Her heart was calling. It was an ancient calling, not so much words as feeling, *instinct,* drive. But following the voice of the heart was no matter to be taken lightly. Some choices were momentous, they had the potential to change everything, forever. Was he feeling that, too? Could he feel that they were standing on the precipice of choosing heart over logic, over mind? Was he trying to get away from that choice?

As if to answer her, Dylan began fishing through one of his shopping bags. He found and unwrapped a ping-pong ball attached to a paddle, and began to play with it, trying to distract Jake. He appeared to be the man least likely to be listening for the ancient language of the heart.

"Let's go to your sister's house," she suggested, resigned. "I'm sure he'll settle more quickly in his own surroundings. He must be ready for a nap. When he goes down, I'll slide out the door. He can wake up to that remote-control helicopter. He won't even know I'm gone."

"Thanks, Katie, my lady."

He wanted her to stay with them.

She glanced at her watch. "I'll call Mrs. Abercrombie and tell her to lock up the store," she said.

"You'll never regret it."

But she already did, because she knew she was getting herself deeper and deeper into this path of the heart. It felt easy and peaceful like a forest walk on a Sunday afternoon, but she wondered how quickly it could turn treacherous, like an encounter with quicksand. Lulled in too far, would she be in real trouble before she realized there was no way to get back out?

"We could still get a puppy," Dylan said wistfully, his expression chasing away her sinister thought of quicksand and danger. He opened the car door for her and she slid in.

Jake crowed, *"SHE!"*

Dylan got in the other side and pulled smoothly into traffic.

"You know what?" Katie said. "Your nephew is not yet two, and he's trying to teach you something."

"Such as?"

"You cannot replace people with things. He wants his *m-o-m,* you can't buy him out of feeling like that. Not with a thousand dollars worth of toys, and not with a puppy."

Dylan shook his head with mock regret. "I hate it when you're right, Katie."

"So, it appears since he can't have his *m-o-m,* he's chosen me as the next best thing. You're stuck with me, Dylan, for the time being. Take me home."

Dylan sighed with satisfaction. "I've been waiting a long time to hear those words from you, Katie, my lady."

"Well, don't get your hopes up. I don't plan to be on the receiving end of a bouquet number two from you."

"I didn't particularly like the bouquet of his number two, either," Dylan said defensively. And then she couldn't help it. She was laughing. And the baby was laughing, and Dylan was laughing, and it felt as if life had handed her the most delightful of gifts when she least expected it. And a woman could not harden her heart against this kind of gift forever.

"I wish we could starve him," Dylan said to Katie, glared at his nephew, and said, "Choo-choo." Jake's mouth remained firmly shut to the spoonful of butterscotch pudding.

They were into day three of looking after Jake. San Francisco was in the soup. His sister was scheduled for yet more surgery. Dylan had resigned himself to the fact his brother-in-law was never coming home, and his sister *liked* the hospital.

No wonder, since her son was a monster.

On the other hand Dylan was aware he had started to hope this funny little escapade he was sharing with Katie could last forever.

Who could have guessed spending time with Katie could be so good? She had tried to leave several times, but Jake had a radar! As soon as the door closed behind Katie, he started to scream and he didn't stop.

The first night, after Jake had awoken in the night to find his beloved mother and his beloved SHE missing, the baby had begun to give his lungs a no-holds-barred workout. Dylan had tried everything. Diaper changes. Cookies. New toys. Bottles. If there had been a place to get a puppy in the middle of the night, he would have tried that, too.

Finally, he had sat outside on the front steps but he had still been able to hear the howls of the baby. When the neighbors' lights started coming on, Dylan had surrendered and called her. He knew he didn't really have to call her. He knew lots of ladies. But he only knew one he trusted so completely. He did not even know quite when or how in the last year of knowing her that Katie had snuck so completely into that zone of trust.

"Hello?" she'd said, her voice soft with sleep. He imagined her all tousled and warm, and suddenly didn't want to get her up, felt as if he was face-to-face with how selfish he really was.

"Sorry, I shouldn't have called."

"Dylan? What's wrong? Is that the baby crying in the background?"

Her voice felt like a life line. "I can't make him stop. Katie, I'm three steps from suicidal."

She laughed.

"Listen to this," he said and held up the phone. Then he'd put it back to his mouth. "Can SHE come?"

Katie had come within minutes, rocked the distraught baby to sleep, sung him some lovely little song that felt as if it would haunt Dylan's heart forever. But every time she tried to put Jake down, he woke, whimpered, wrapped his fist in her hair. Finally, she fell asleep in the rocking chair beside his crib.

When Dylan crept in and covered her with a blanket, he was not prepared for the welling of emotion he felt as he looked into the gentle beauty of her face.

He knew people—people like him—could look at a girl like her and miss all the things that were most important in human nature: it wasn't about being able to stop traffic or your beauty, or the perfect red-carpet twirl.

It was about surviving your sorrows and allowing them to make you better instead of worse. He could learn something from her, from how her gentle spirit had remained intact. Guarded to be sure, but intact nonetheless. Katie was still willing to risk *giving,* and living, a kind of quiet courage about her that was incredibly beautiful.

The next day, while Jake napped, she had left for long enough to pack a little overnight bag and come back. She was now set up in his sister's guest room.

Dylan had done some of the most exciting things a man could do. He had been attracted to speed and to adrenaline his entire life.

So how was it, playing in the backyard, digging in a flowerbed, introducing Jake to the joy of worms and watching Katie brush dirt off his nephew's face, could be more satisfying than that?

Dylan had been to some of the world's most enviable parties. He had schmoozed with the Oscar winners, the rock stars, the Olympians.

So how was it, having a quiet glass of wine with her, when Jake finally surrendered to sleep was better than that? How was it that to hear her tell him a story about a customer at the flower shop was funnier and better than hearing a famous comedian's hilarious rendition of his week in treatment?

He had run marathons and accepted trophies, but when he had gotten on a bike attached to a little baby carrier on wheels, and Katie had ridden beside him, deliberately hitting every puddle at full speed, shining with light and laughter, it was then that he had felt completely fulfilled.

Now this. A silly moment with butterscotch pudding and a baby and her, better than the five-star meals he'd had in some of the best restaurants in the world.

"Try the airplane," Katie said.

Despite all his best cajoling, Jake's mouth remained stubbornly shut to him. Jake swatted crankily at the spoon and it added to the butterscotch pudding in his hair, on his ears and down the front of his shirt. And there was some on the baby, too!

Dylan surrendered the spoon to Katie, and Jake opened his mouth eagerly, like a greedy little bird.

"Everything you put in there has to come out the other end," Dylan reminded her.

"Dylan, stop it. You're being gross."

"Realistic," he argued, even though the truth was he took a rather fiendish delight grossing her out. It was so easy to do, and it played havoc with her carefully erected barricades. "Hopefully by recycling time, Sam will be home."

"Hopefully," she agreed weakly, and he knew she dreaded Sam coming home as much as he did. "Though, really, Dylan we should clean up the house before he comes home."

Over the last few days, Dylan had opened every toy he had bought. His sister's house was littered with toys: jack-in-the-box, foam rubber footballs, stuffed animals, building blocks. They'd crashed remote control cars into his sister's furniture and got finger-paint on her couch. Dylan was unabashed in the fact he was enjoying the toys far more than the baby who seemed to have a fascination with the boxes they came in.

"Since my sister likes to address all my complaints about the position I have been forced into with 'Suck it up, buttercup,' I am not cleaning up her house."

Katie laughed.

"And the next time she asks me to get Sam tickets to a Blue Jays game, you know what she's getting? 'Outta luck, pickup truck.'"

He liked making Katie laugh. And grossing her out. He liked teasing her. He even had to admit he liked showing off for her. The bottom line was he liked sharing this experience with her.

Somewhere he remembered hearing that dogs and babies were true judges of character, and he could clearly see that was true in the way Jake had taken to Kate.

Not just taken to her, but was possessive of her, unwilling to share. Tonight he was wondering if the baby was ever going to go to sleep so he could have Katie to himself. It had become such a wonderful part of his day. Katie relaxed on the couch beside him, sipping wine.

It occurred to him he should have a plan. That he wanted things to move forward. Sooner or later that baby was going down. Then what? Ah, maybe the baby had judged the nefariousness of his own character a little too well!

You had to be careful with a girl like Katie. Things he would do with another woman, almost without a thought, would have repercussions with her.

Still, could he kiss her? Just one little brush of his lips

against hers? That kind of kiss a guy gave a girl that meant thank you? That expressed "I don't know how I could have done this without you."

The problem was he'd had very little practice at that kind of kiss. When he kissed a girl it was a prelude to the main show.

And Katie wasn't that kind of girl. Kissing her would complicate both their worlds unbearably. It would be a dumb, dumb thing to do.

So of course he did it. Right in between his nephew gulping down bites of butterscotch pudding, not even waiting for the right moment, he leaned over and surrendered to the utter temptation of her plump lips. He kissed her.

She tasted of something he was not sure he had ever tasted before. Given her understated look, her mouth tasted wild and clean, like rain-soaked mist over an untamed mountain.

There were a thousand things she could have done, and he was aware that he was prepared for each of them: for her lips to remain prudish underneath his, for her to hit him, throw pudding on him, get up and run—

But Katie's lips parted under his, warm and delicious, as if she had known her whole life this moment would come, as if she had waited, a desert flower opening for the rain.

Her kiss was not the predatory kiss of Heather, nor the promising kiss of a thousand other girls he had kissed. It was not reckless or abandoned.

Her lips on his were faintly thoughtful, curious, undeniably sensual in the loveliest of ways, like having silk drawn over freshly bathed skin.

He reeled back from her, stunned by what he had discovered.

And what he had known all along.

He had known all along that beneath that demure exterior, she was something special, that her treasures were hidden. No, there were no gaudy displays for the entire world to see, a man had to go deeper, trust his heart to lead him, follow his instincts to the place where her true beauty would be unveiled.

What he'd discovered was that he wanted to be a guy who was worthy of discovering her deepest secrets, her treasure. What he discovered in that single tantalizing kiss was that he was tired of shallow people and superficial relationships, he was weary to the bone of the games he had played. They had emptied him, and something about her moist mouth under his promised to do the exact opposite.

To fill the emptiness within him until he overflowed.

He wanted what he had tasted: depth, mystery, complexity, companionship, integrity. It seemed impossible that her mouth, in that brief encounter that had left him hungry for more, had told him each of those things, but it had.

Or maybe he had seen each of those things in the gorgeous depths of those ever-changing eyes, one second green, the next gold, for as long as he could remember.

And maybe he had always known he was afraid his sister had been right that day. That he had gone so far down a wrong road that he could not be worthy of a girl like Katie. Just like her ex-husband had not been worthy.

But even thinking of that, he knew he was not anything like her ex had been. Because he *wanted* to be the one who was there for her when life turned unexpectedly sour, when she needed someone strong to lean on. It felt like the job he'd been born to do.

Oh sure, he had played the field and availed himself of every perk that came with his career and fame and money. But he had never, ever pretended with anyone.

He had never claimed he would be more than he was. He had never said he was ready for commitment. He had always been totally honest about where each and every relationship was going: nowhere.

But in her lips he had tasted somewhere. And it was a somewhere he had never been. A place where the loneliness he had somehow come to live with promised to disappear like mist under a gentle sun, a place that invited him to be more, better, deeper, truer.

A place that invited him to know another person for the pleasure and richness of knowing them to their soul, not for whatever use they might be to him.

He leaped back from all the things he had tasted in her lips so swiftly he knocked over the kitchen chair. He couldn't be trusted with anything as precious, as real, as Katie Pritchard. As she'd already pointed out he couldn't even be trusted with a houseplant!

On the other hand, he'd just been trusted with a baby. Maybe there was more to him than he'd ever given himself credit for.

"Dylan," she said primly, "I don't think you should do that again."

"No kidding," he muttered, and went and busied himself assembling the wagon he had bought earlier. He liked things that came with instructions. Even things that appeared to people to be daredevil like skydiving or riding motorcycles really weren't.

They came with a complete set of rigid rules. If you followed those rules exactly, you got an exact result. Problems only resulted when the rules were broken, modified, stretched.

All his life people had seen him as a daredevil.

And there was some truth to that. He liked the rush of adrenaline that came from pushing the envelope. He liked the adventure of trying new things. He liked how activity could make a man feel full to the top.

And then one tiny little kiss toppled the whole thing, and made him feel empty and look into the face an uncomfortable truth.

He wasn't fearless at all.

He had filled all the spaces around him with things, successes, activities. He had tried to fill up every hole inside of him, to plug the leaks in his soul. To run from the fact that he had become afraid of the one thing that could truly fill him up.

Dylan McKinnon was fearful of love.

He had believed in it once. He had always thought one day he would be done living fast and having fun and he would find *the* girl to settle down with. He had assumed he would have a wonderful relationship, like the one his mother and father had enjoyed. Theirs had been a relationship of complete respect. Of laughter. Of companionship. You could not be in the same room as them and not sense the connection: the tender brush of hands, the meeting of eyes.

And then his mother had become ill. It had seemed innocuous at first, maybe even funny: her curling iron in the fridge, her saying bum when she meant bun. But it had deteriorated at a horrifying speed, stove burners left on, wandering through the neighborhood in the dead of night. Dylan remembered the day he'd known it was never going to be the same. He'd been in her car with her, and she'd looked at him, called him by his father's name, and announced calmly she couldn't remember the difference between the gas pedal and the brake.

Still, even though at some level he understood his father could not cope with it, and that it was no longer safe for him to try, he felt furious when his father made the decision to put her in the nursing home, a fury that deepened when his father became reluctant to visit her.

This had been his model for love, his model *for better or worse,* and it had fallen apart when the *worse* arrived.

Dylan felt as if he grieved a mother who was not yet dead, and a dream—his own dream—of a relationship that had never been born.

Katie was the best of things, because a little seedling of hope came to life inside him around her. And she was the worst of things, because a little seedling of hope came to life inside of him around her.

She required him to look at the thing he most wanted to deny. Dylan McKinnon, daredevil, fearless, was being ruled by fear. He was afraid to love.

He had achieved it all. He had money, success, fame. Until he'd met Katie he'd been able to outrun the fact that for all that, he was empty.

Because he had rejected and run from that one thing that made a man truly rich.

Love.

CHAPTER SEVEN

THERE were probably words, moments, that people regretted to their graves, Katie decided. And she knew exactly which ones she would be contemplating with deep remorse on her death bed. After that spontaneous kiss over butterscotch pudding had she really said, "Dylan, I don't think you should do that again"?

Katie sighed. She really had. And he hadn't even attempted to do it again. Which was annoying, because it was just a little late in life for Dylan McKinnon to start being a gentleman! She knew he wanted to kiss her again.

They had been in this house together, manning the baby battle stations with Jake for days. The house itself filled her with yearning, not because it was a beautiful house, though it was. But because she could feel the love of the family that lived here.

It was in the wedding pictures proudly displayed, in the baby pictures of the three of them. It was in the funny little notes Sam and Tara left on the fridge for each other, it was in the flowers that he'd sent her while he was away on business.

There was one photo in particular, of just Sam and Tara, and Sam was looking at his wife with such pride and delight and hunger that it felt like spying to even look at it.

Katie was well aware that Dylan watched her when he thought she wasn't looking, and she was astounded that his look was not that different than the look of his brother-in-law looking at his wife.

She was well aware of the carefully masked heat in Dylan's eyes when he looked at her lips. She was well aware of how his hand brushed hers far more than was necessary, lingering. She was well aware of the beat of her own heart, her own secret looks at him, the roller-coaster rush in her stomach that seemed to be permanent.

She was exhausted with tension, in his sister's guest bedroom, wide awake, despite the late hour and the fact they had had an absolutely unbelievable day with Jake. Who knew a tiny little baby took so much energy?

Who knew everything about a baby was hard? From bathing him, to trying to get him into his cute little clothes? Who knew a baby could cry without stopping until his eyes ran dry and just the howls remained?

And who knew that same baby could cause your heart to feel as if it would burst it was so filled with tenderness? Who knew that a tiny little scrap of humanity, one who didn't even have words, could be so funny you could hurt from laughing so hard?

Who knew that a baby could show you everything that was real about a man's heart? The baby could show you how a man could be in a situation totally alien to him, frustrating, challenging, aggravating, and remain patient, strong, capable, good-humored. Dylan's disguise was that he was a playboy. In reality, the man was a natural-born daddy.

Katie was seeing him through that filter, and it filled her with the most terrifying longing. That longing had only been intensified by his kiss.

His kiss, in the wildly unromantic atmosphere of butterscotch pudding, had taken her completely by surprise. It had come out of nowhere. One second she'd been feeding the baby, the next she had been falling into the unknown abyss that was love.

But wasn't that where most life-altering events came from? Seemingly from nowhere? Deciding to go one place instead of another, meeting a stranger's eyes on the bus, answering an email, saying yes to the friend who had been bugging you about the blind date. An ordinary life, suddenly on an intercept course with destiny.

Destiny.

She was twenty-six years old and she had found out something brand-new. When you kissed a person, there was an exchange of energy: some mysterious force leapt from them to you, and you saw or felt things you had never seen or felt before.

This had not been the case with her ex-husband, which she now realized, had she been more experienced, she would have read as a warning. The fact that Marcus's kiss had been so unrevealing should have been a big red stop sign.

Because when Dylan's lips had touched hers she had known things about him: felt his strength, his heart, his soul. And she had felt her own destiny.

The thing was, a person always had choices. Destiny was a road with many branches off it. You didn't have to take each one that beckoned. You could choose the safe road, predictable, pleasantly scenic, well marked, the destination clear.

Who wouldn't choose that one, rather than the barely discernible path that climbed steeply upward, through forests that undoubtedly held monsters, hazards, messy places that were terribly hard to traverse, if they could be traversed at all?

Who would choose a path that's only promise was that you would be challenged, tossed and turned, your comfort zone a distant memory? Who would choose the path that made your heart race with fear and discovery and exertion? Who would choose the path that made you feel as though you had lost your map, your direction, your compass? Who would choose such a way?

But only one way rewarded the intrepid soul who had chosen it with the pure exhilaration of the mountaintop, and that was never going to be the safe road.

The safe road led her where she had already been.

The sad truth was, when she had married Marcus, Katie had known somewhere in herself, she was *settling*, taking less than she deserved, so much less than what she wanted. She had been so desperate to make all her dreams come true, that she had become determined to make her husband fit *her* dream. She had thought once they had the baby it would all start to work out. She had ignored the clues he had given her that they didn't want the same things. Marcus had wanted career and financial success, a family had been secondary to him. She had missed that until it was too late.

Had life given her another chance? Or was she deluding herself that a man like Dylan, confident, successful, gorgeous, charming could ever care for a girl like her, plain and ordinary? No, not *care*. It was more than obvious he *cared*. And she could *settle* again, try to make that enough. Or she could take the chance to find out if he could *love* her.

But if sending his flowers was any indication, Dylan didn't have a particularly good track record.

On the other hand, neither did she.

And if she did not want to spend her last moment on earth filled with regret, wondering what could have been if she had just showed a little more courage, a touch more spunk, she was going to have to do something.

Opportunity knocked. They were in this house together now. Sam and Tara could arrive home at any time.

Their adventure would be over.

How did she want it to end? Could she prevent it from ending? The thoughts were so audacious it frightened her to think about them, let alone to contemplate acting on them. But to be with Dylan, she was going to have to find out if she could be as fearless as he could.

Taking a deep breath, she got up, opened her door, crept down the hall to where he slept in the master bedroom.

Her hand went to the doorknob, and she almost fainted at what she was thinking of doing. Quickly she scurried down the hall to the kitchen, turned on the light. She would make cocoa. She would think this through before she did anything drastic, irreversible.

She looked down at herself and groaned. She had made one quick trip home to pick up her car, check on the store, gather a few items of clothing and toiletries. What had she been thinking when she had chosen these pajamas? Not of seduction, obviously.

They were her spring pajamas: drawstring pants, too

large button-down shirt, embossed flowers, bells of Ireland, which stood for good luck. Which, she realized with a sigh, was very different than getting lucky.

Good luck said with a certain intonation could even mean the exact opposite, a sarcastic prediction of failure.

She was not sexy. She could not do lingerie and lace with any degree of comfort. Lace *scratched* for goodness' sake.

Though at the moment she would have made the sacrifice if it would have given her the confidence to open that closed bedroom door, go through it, whisper Dylan awake with a kiss on his whisker-roughened face.

She opened a cupboard in search of cocoa, sadly aware this could be her life, past, present and future: sleepless nights with cocoa as her only companion.

"Hi, there."

She dropped the cocoa on the floor, spun to look at him. Life was so unfair.

He was wearing drawstring pajama bottoms, plaid, not so unlike the unisex models she sported. But on him they were absolutely tantalizing. They rode low, stretched over his hips to show the tautness of his belly. His chest was bare, and so beautiful it made her feel almost faint with wanting: to touch him, to hold him, to *have* him.

All this time she'd been resisting. If only he'd known the only thing he had to do was take off his shirt and she would have succumbed. He stooped and picked up the dropped cocoa, set it on the counter, as if he was afraid to hand it to her, afraid to touch her.

It seemed *trashy* to her, to be feeling this way, and at the same time she was aware of the wonderful freedom of not caring about labels, about what anyone thought.

She was aware of *liking* the compelling feeling inside her, wanting to follow it where it led.

To take the pathway, uncharted, that led to the mountaintop.

"Hi," she stammered, turning back to the open cupboard, pretending to study its contents, when in fact she didn't know if she was looking at peanut butter or marshmallows. And didn't care, either. "I couldn't sleep."

"Me, neither. Funny, because I'm exhausted."

She sneaked another look at him. Her heart thudded wildly. What had she thought she was going to do when she'd had her hand on the doorknob? She licked her lips.

"Don't do that, Katie, my lady."

"What?" she stammered.

"Lick your lips. Please don't do that." His voice was hoarse.

She should just say okay, but she was in the grip of something bigger than the logic that had controlled her for her entire life. She was on the mountain path. So instead she said, surprised at how sultry her voice was, "Why not?"

He ran a hand through the tousled locks of his dark hair. "Because it makes you look so sexy it hurts."

She stared at him. No lace. No lingerie.

It washed over her unexpectedly. Pure courage. A desire to take the other path, no matter how treacherous it was, no matter how many surprises it held.

She went to him.

His eyes never left her. She stopped in front of him, closed her eyes, breathed in the deep glorious scent of the mountaintop. She put her hand on his chest, and he covered it with his own and then placed the other one on the small of her back and propelled her into him.

His body was lean, strong, his naked skin the texture of silk. She sighed against him. It felt as though her whole life she had waited for this exact moment. It was a moment of pure homecoming, her body pressed so close to his that she absorbed the beat of his heart through her skin, and it drummed her own life song.

She hadn't just reached the mountaintop. She *belonged* on it. She was worthy of soaring with eagles.

She tilted her head up, and he took his hand that had been on the small of her back, caressed her cheek, looked at her with a wonder that reflected her own. He scraped his thumb across her lips, exploring, the look of wonder deepening in his eyes.

She nuzzled his thumb, then nipped it, watched the surprise and then the welcome darken his eyes. They sparked with the dangerous and absolutely delightful light of desire.

She knew he sincerely did not know she was in the world's ugliest pajamas. When he looked at her like that, she felt as if he saw her, she felt as if it was the first time anyone had truly seen her.

"You told me not to do this again," he said hoarsely.

"I know. And I meant it."

"Tease," he choked out.

"No. It's my turn. I'm going to do the kissing this time, Dylan."

She reached up and took his lips with her own. She tasted, she explored, she delighted, she discovered. He held back, pliant, letting her have her moment, surrendering to her female power.

And then he held back no longer. With a moan of suppressed desire, he tangled his hands in her hair, drew her lips more aggressively to his own. He tasted her back, his hunger fierce, his desire unleashed.

His kiss took her to her own fullness. It returned to the wild call in her that had been tamed, it set unlocked what had been captive. It brought her to the place where she was, finally, free: no thought, no plan, no predictions and especially no fear.

She was the eagle, soaring, proud, hungry, fierce, independent, majestic.

As her lips drank him, her hands explored, greedy with wanting to know every ripple of muscle, every hard plain of skin, every hair on his arms and chest. She felt a delicious sense of the sacred: that she was obeying the ancient call.

It was the voice that called without words. It commanded one man and one woman to be together. Only a union so intense and so intimate and so powerful was worthy of what it produced, the life force being celebrated, honored, passed from one generation to the next. This was the ancient call that guaranteed the survival of something so frail and so flawed as the human race.

Katie wanted it. She wanted the mountaintop. And in this moment she had no care what it cost her to get there. Like a climber on Everest, her focus had narrowed to one thing, the price of having it was no longer of consequence.

When he scooped her up in his arms, she felt his strength, knew he had committed just as she had. And she was glad.

* * *

Dylan McKinnon had probably kissed a thousand women, so many that the experiences blurred together, a casual coming together of human beings to meet a mutual need.

Now he was aware of being in the grip of something so powerful and so sacred that it made him ashamed of what he had accepted before.

This thing with Katie was physical, and yet it was more than that, her spirit rushing out to meet his in a way that was all encompassing, that promised to bring him to a place he had never been before.

Kissing Katie made him feel as if he was a man who had crossed the desert, finding oasis after oasis, only to know now each had been a mirage, each had given the illusion of a thirst slaked, but each illusion had actually made his thirst grow.

It was not a thirst for sex.

It was a thirst for connection.

It was a thirst for completion.

He lifted her into his arms and felt her slightness, felt how wonderfully she fit with him, felt something in her open, her cautiousness gone, and behind the wall of it, an oasis, a garden so full of vibrant life and delight, that a man could satisfy his thirst there forever.

He carried her down the hall and through the door of the guest bedroom. He laid her on the bed, stood above her and marveled at the fullness of her lips, the hooded desire in her eyes, the way her hair scattered across the pillow.

Her eyes never leaving his, she found her top button and undid it, and then the next and the next.

He wanted to ask her if she was sure, but he was

afraid words might break the spell, the enchantment, they were both in. Instead he lay down beside her, stilled her hand, undid the last two buttons himself.

But he did not open her shirt. Instead he thought of the tremendous gift she was giving him. Instead he wondered if he was worthy.

And suddenly he knew a terrible truth.

It was absolutely the wrong time to think of his mother. And yet he knew a simple and wondrous thing, even if the timing was awful. His mother, as he had known her, was gone. But what she had taught him was not gone. Who she had been—a woman of absolute integrity, would be with him forever.

That was how she would go on, and that was how he could honor the memory of the strong incredible woman she had been.

By doing the right thing. The thing she would have approved of. The thing she would have been proud of him for. The thing his sister had called *decent*.

If he took Katie like this, he was not the man his mother had always hoped he would be. Not even close. If he took the way he had been taking this past year, he was desecrating the life lessons his mother had given him, and even worse desecrating what Katie offered.

His mother would go on *through* him, through how he lived, the choices he made. And that choice had to be to live with honor, no matter how hard that was.

And in this moment it was plenty hard.

He had always entered into liaisons thoughtlessly. No thought of the future, no thought of what it meant, certainly no thought of the damage he might cause another person.

But to damage Katie?

To take her greatest gift without thinking what it meant to him? And to her? And to them? To enter into this most sacred of unions with her and not have a plan for tomorrow and the next day and the day beyond that.

He groaned out loud.

"What's wrong?"

"Katie, nothing. Everything."

"You have a look on your face," she said tentatively. "I've seen it before."

He reached to her, and began doing the buttons back up.

"Dylan," she said, her voice a whimper of wanting that nearly killed him, that threatened to overcome the discipline it was taking to do her shirt back up.

Lust had undone her buttons. Love did them back up.

Love. He loved her. And he hated it that he loved her. What, of all the nebulous things in the universe, was more unpredictable than that? Harder to control?

"That's where I've seen that look before," she said softly. "Sadness. It's when you choose that bouquet of flowers every Friday."

The flowers he brought to his mother.

"Who are the flowers for?" she whispered.

This was not what he wanted to give Katie. His baggage, his burdens. If they ever made love he wanted it to be free and joyous.

His sister had kept warning him to deal with his "stuff." Naturally, he had thought she should mind her own business, and felt that dealing with "stuff" was for wimps who had not perfected the art of shutting down their feelings by pursuing manly arts like drinking beer, chasing girls and riding motorcycles.

Now, though, that stuff had come back to bite him. The door was open, and thoughts of his mother and father crept through. He had always thought it was never ending.

And then his mother slipping into what they would later learn was early onset Alzheimer's. And his father giving up. Putting her in a home. Meeting Dylan's fury with resignation and stubbornness.

Dylan took his mother flowers every week, looked for some sign that she recognized him, cared. When it was obvious she had nothing left to give him, he tried to think of things to give her. He read her the poetry she had so enjoyed when he was young. He bought her movies and magazines. But not a spark of recognition, not a hint of who she used to be. He was not even sure his father went to see her anymore.

In fact, last time he had gone by his father's he had seen a brochure for a cruise lying open on the kitchen table. A cruise. His suspicions that his father was seeing someone else had deepened, but not been discussed.

Now, looking at Katie, for the first time he felt the smallest glimmer of understanding for his father. To see those eyes, in this moment so filled with love, staring at him blankly, without recognition, that would be a kind of death in itself.

To remember a woman who'd ridden her bike through puddles, and tackled diaper changes and butterscotch pudding, whose laughter could put the sun to shame, while looking at a shell, would be the most devastating kind of pain.

He didn't want to understand his father!

And maybe, really, he had no desire to understand himself, either. Or at least not the part that would be weak instead of strong.

What if he had inherited the gene that brought on his mother's illness? What if asking Katie to share a future with him meant that someday she would be looking at him and no longer knowing who he was? What if it meant she would have to make some of those hard, hard choices that his father had made?

Was that what love did? Asked people to make choices so hard they could tear the heart right out of them? Love could change cruelly and without warning, so was it better to not risk it at all?

He looked at Katie, kissed her finger, put it to his lips. God, he'd been playing a game with her all along.

All he'd had to say, from the very beginning, was he was sorry life had delivered her some blows she did not deserve. No, instead of keeping it simple he'd had to make everything complicated, play with her, kid himself about his motivations. He'd allowed himself to be driven to prove his own decency, now he wondered if he had not proved the exact opposite instead.

What was decent about a man trying to make love to a woman he had offered no commitment to? Especially if that woman was like Katie?

"I can't do this," he said softly. "I'm sorry." The decent thing after all.

But she didn't react with any appreciation for his sacrifice or his decency!

She gave him one killing look, scrambled out of the bed and turned and marched out of the room. Apparently uncaring that she was in her pajamas and her feet were bare, she went out the front door of his sister's house, slammed the door behind her. He heard her car start up and pull away.

He lay there for a long time with his eyes open. They felt like they were burning. He tried to choke back whatever emotion he was feeling. He was glad he had not told her he bought that weekly bouquet for his mother. There was no point in feeling even more vulnerable than he did.

He resented Katie. Nothing with her ever went the way he planned it. Not wooing her, not making love to her, not apologizing to her, nothing.

Having a relationship with her would be a constant challenge. He would have to make a habit of being thoughtful and nice, completely honest, *giving*. He had obviously pulled back just in the nick of time.

But if that was true why did he feel so sick inside? No, not just sick, bereft, as if he was suddenly being swamped by every single feeling he'd ever refused to have.

But if there was one thing Daredevil Dylan McKinnon had become it was an absolute expert at outrunning feelings.

CHAPTER EIGHT

THE DOOR to her shop opened, and Katie jumped, whirled to see who was coming in her door. She had to quit doing that. It wasn't going to be Dylan. Two weeks had passed since that night they had almost made love.

She tried to stop hoping he was coming, tried to stop hoping that one of these days he would breeze in, and say, "Katie, my lady, what do you think of the jacket?"

Or "Katie, my lady, come and swim with me and the dolphins."

Maybe he would drop by on Friday, the day he had always come in to choose the blossoms for his special bouquet?

On the verge of intimacy, she reminded herself, she had asked him about that bouquet. And he had kept his secret. A man with secrets was *always* a bad thing.

She was divorced, and she had not missed her ex-husband the way she missed Dylan. In fact, underneath the shame of failing at marriage, she had been relieved to leave the tension and uncertainty and loneliness of sharing a life with Marcus far behind her.

Still, she was tense and uncertain now! It was a blessing that things had not gone further between her and Dylan, that he had come to his senses that night. Because if she could feel like this over absolutely nothing—which is what had gone on between them—how would she feel if anything more had happened?

How would she feel if she had said yes to motorcycle rides and dinners for two and skating through the park? Much worse. Yes, she had been very wise to beat off his advances.

Maybe, a little voice chided her, *had she said yes she would feel as though she had lived, as if she would be one of those lucky few people, who on their deathbeds, had no regrets.*

Maybe she was hoping for a second chance to live, maybe that's why she could not stop her heart from leaping every time the door opened, from turning to look, hope nearly strangling her, just wanting to see him and hear his voice.

Not that that was going to be enough anymore. Not now that she had tasted his lips, not now that she had touched his skin; not now that she had unbuttoned her blouse to him.

Katie watched the door squeak open. A strikingly lovely woman struggled through in a wheelchair, one leg, plaster-encased from toe to hip, stretched out in front of her. Katie would have come out from behind the counter to assist her, except she recognized her from the photographs at Tara and Sam's house. This was Jake's mother. This was Dylan's sister.

Her first horrible thought was that something had happened to Dylan. That's why she hadn't seen him. That's why he was no longer running at one o'clock every day. As upset about the foibles of love as Katie herself, he'd wrapped his motorcycle around a telephone pole. They'd found Katie's name on some papers on his desk. No! They were coming to order the flowers for—

Katie cut herself off sharply. The face she was looking at was not the face of a woman planning a funeral. Tara's face was cheerful and filled with warmth.

She rolled up to the counter, put out her hand. Katie leaned across and took it, aware she was being regarded with interest that was more than casual.

"I found some of your things at my place," Tara said, and passed Katie a bag.

Katie grabbed the bag, peeked in it at some of her most personal items and stuffed it behind the counter. She was reminded she had left in a hurry.

"It's not what you think!" she squeaked.

"What do I think?" Tara asked mildly.

"That Dylan and I—" She could feel herself blushing scarlet.

"Of course I don't think that!" Tara said kindly. "I could believe it of my brother, but not of you. I can tell by looking at you, you aren't that kind of girl."

Katie found herself being studied intently.

"Decent," Tara proclaimed happily, as if that compliment rated right up there with *beautiful*.

Kate decided it would not be in her best interest to point out she had very nearly not been a decent girl at all.

But looking at Tara, she decided what Dylan's sister meant, but was too kind to say, was that Katie Pritchard was not Dylan's kind of girl.

As in a candidate for a professional football team's cheerleading squad.

"I just wanted to thank you for all you did for Dylan

and Jakie when I had my accident. The thought of Dylan with Jake by himself…" She shook her head, and rolled her eyes.

"Dylan's actually very good with the baby," Katie said, and then could have kicked herself for defending him, especially when the light of interest in his sister's eyes deepened even further.

"Oh, I know he's good with Jake," Tara said. "I just don't know if the house would have still been standing if he'd been left entirely to his own devices. As it was, I had to give three boxes of toys away, and have been scraping butterscotch pudding off the cabinets since I got home."

Katie had meant to look after the butterscotch pudding. She was reminded again that she had left in a hurry.

"Who liked the toys more," Tara asked, "Dylan or Jake?"

"Dylan," Katie said without hesitation, and then found herself chuckling along with Tara. It was the first time in two weeks she'd laughed.

"I bet that ridiculous remote control helicopter was his favorite. It's my husband, Sam's favorite, too. Or was. I can't tell you how overjoyed I was when Sam got it stuck in that high chandelier above the stairwell."

She smiled with indulgence for her husband that revealed such love that Katie felt a pang of envy. She had seen that love, *felt* it in their home.

"I wanted to send flowers to thank you, but when Dylan said not to bother, that you had a flower shop, I decided to come see if you wanted to go for lunch instead. I left Jake at Dylan's office. Just for revenge I loaded up his baby pack with butterscotch pudding and the fire engine with the extra loud siren."

Katie found herself laughing again. Truly, she wanted to say no. What was the point of tangling her life with his any more than she already had? It would just make life awkward for him. On the other hand, he had said not to bother sending her flowers? Jerk! What did she care if life was awkward for him?

When she was busy mooning over imagined conversations about jacket sleeves and dolphin swimming she'd do well to remember this side of him.

Besides, Katie felt herself liking his sister. She had laughed more in the past two minutes than she had in the past two weeks. Why not go for lunch? Friendships with women were so wonderfully *safe*.

"I'd love to have lunch with you," she decided impulsively. "Let me just leave a few instructions with Mrs. Abercrombie and we can go."

As they passed his office, Katie pushing the wheelchair, she saw Dylan standing at the window with Jake. He scowled when he saw his sister with her. Tara stuck out her tongue at him, while Katie looked determinedly straight ahead. Still, even through the windows, they could hear Jake's excited shouts of *SHE*.

Once they were past the obstacle of the window, though, Katie noticed the weather was beautiful, a fact Katie had not even registered about the day until now. Given the gorgeous sunshine they chose a little café with an outdoor eating area just down the block from the flower shop and Dylan's office. They ordered wraps, sipped chai tea and basked in the warmth.

"Have you noticed Dylan seems a little, um, cranky?" Tara said, when her food had arrived.

"I haven't seen Dylan," Katie said proudly.

"You haven't?"

"No. Him standing at the window is the closest I've been to him in two weeks."

"But why?"

"Surely you know your brother well enough to know his—" she tried to think of a word, and said carefully "—his dalliances are temporary."

"You are not a dalliance!"

Almost. Katie had almost been a dalliance. Ashamed to admit, even to herself, how she wished she had been, even if he had secrets. Even if it did last only one night. Surely she couldn't hurt more than she did right now. And then she would have had that experience to cradle in her lonely bed at night.

Anyway, being a dalliance would have been much easier to handle than being rejected right at the moment of truth!

"Did you have a fight?" Tara asked. "I wondered if you'd left my place on bad terms. You left so many things there."

"We didn't have a fight." *He rejected me.* A knock-down, drag-'em-out screaming match seemed as if it would have been preferable.

"Hmm. Well, something's eating him. He's gone into overdrive. Given that what most people would consider overdrive is his normal, his overdrive is maniacal."

"What do you mean?"

"Let's see—he's taking up rock climbing, just on the wall for now, he tells me, but planning a trip to the Rockies this summer. Then I saw him drive by with a kayak on top of his car, he invited us to watch him in a motorcycle race this past weekend and I heard on the news last night he's leaving for a camel trek across the Sahara in a few days. On Friday."

"A camel trek?" Katie said, incredulous.

"I tried to ask him about it this morning, but he just growled at me that he'd send a postcard. Where on earth do you send a postcard from in the Sahara?"

"The Desert Oasis and Belly-Dancing Emporium," Katie guessed cynically.

"Strangely, as far as I can tell, he doesn't have one of his bimbos on his arm right now."

Katie tried to keep her relief from her face. It was none of her business who he had or didn't have on his arm. She just had to pray when he did have a new object of his interest, he wasn't going to send that nice-to-meet-you bouquet through her!

If he did, she'd have no choice but to use yellow carnations to express her disappointment and disdain. And maybe a little monkshood to warn the poor girl a deadly foe was near.

Tara looked troubled. "I don't know about this playboy thing he does. He was never like that before Mom got sick."

"Your mom is sick?" Katie asked slowly. His mother was sick? "I'm sorry. I thought she had passed on."

Why had he let her believe that? But when she thought back on it, he had never said his mother was dead.

"Dylan told me she was gone."

Tara nodded sadly. "She is gone. Alzheimer's. My dad made a decision to put her in a care facility. It's the best, Highlands, over on the Westside, but there's still no mistaking it's an institution. Dylan was against it, to put it mildly. He offered to hire a nurse to care for her at home. But the thought of someone else living in their home twenty-four hours a day did not sit well with Dad. It's not just that he's a very private person.

"I think having Mom at home, in the shape she was in, was like being stabbed in the heart over and over again for Dad. She was becoming a stranger, not the woman he had loved for thirty-five years.

"Those last months when she was at home were absolutely frightening. She was leaving the stove on, breaking things. Sometimes she'd go out at night and wander around the neighborhood in her nightgown. She even found a hidden set of car keys one day and went for a drive. The police brought her home. Thank God she didn't kill someone or get lost somewhere where she might have been in danger."

"Oh, I'm so sorry," Katie said. "I can't imagine how dreadful that must be for your whole family." Dylan hadn't told her. He had not trusted her with the wound to his own heart.

It seemed that little secret hope she had been harboring, that he would come around, that there might be something there, was shriveling up inside her and dying. He had not shown her anything about him that *mattered* after all.

Or maybe in a way he had. Every week, coming in, faithfully choosing the most beautiful flowers, his secret bouquet.

Katie knew suddenly, who they were for, remembered the sadness in his face as he had chosen them. Then she remembered that same sadness marring his handsome features when he had been about to surrender to her.

And then pulled back.

"It's been hard on everyone. Dylan is all stiff upper lip, but he's been terribly unforgiving of my father. Then, to make everything worse, one of the neighbors, a friend of Mom's, has been really there for Dad. I suspect it's been platonic, but they were planning to go on a cruise together, and Dylan got wind of it. Poor Dad canceled the cruise, but Dylan still won't take his calls.

"Anyway, Dylan's gone-wild-with-girls thing seemed to have coincided with my mother's hospitalization. Not to mention the other craziness. I thought bungee jumping was the worst of it. Oh, no, he has to one-up himself and ride a camel across the desert!"

Katie saw Tara's very real love and concern for her brother. And she began to see his pulling away from her that night might not have been about her at all. It hadn't been about any of the things she had tormented herself with in the last weeks.

It had not been because she was not beautiful enough. It had not been because she had said or done the wrong thing at the wrong time. It had not been because she was divorced, *flawed*. Those were her own insecurities.

It wasn't her he'd been afraid to surrender to; it was love. Love, the beautiful rose with the terrible thorns.

"When did your mother become ill?" Katie asked softly.

"It started about three years ago, it's been about a year now since she went to Highlands."

Katie could have guessed that, without Tara confirming it. A year ago, just when she had opened The Flower Girl. His girl-a-month campaign just getting under way.

"Dylan," his sister said, "has always been popular, to be sure. But when he was playing ball he had a single-ness of focus that was unreal. No relationships then, or at least nothing serious. It was the same when he started the business. He's always been very intensely focused on his career. There was no time for romance. I used to nag him about it. I wanted so badly for him to meet the right girl, have a family. He's such a great guy. I didn't want him to miss everything that was best in life. Though, after watching him perform this year it's been a case of 'Be careful what you wish for.' My goodness, I have never seen such an aggravating line-up of empty-headed bimbos in my whole life."

But Katie got it. *Women who required nothing of him.*

And when he had met one who had required more of him, he had backed away.

And Katie had to admit, even at the height of Dylan's girl-a-month campaign, there was nothing sneaky about him, unless she counted the fact he had tried—almost desperately—to make her believe he was a worse person than he was. He had done what he had done but without pretense, without leading anyone on, without making any promises.

She knew all that, because she had said it all for him with flowers.

It was probably a mark of her own weakness that Katie was seeing that as a kind of honor system.

"I think he's decided superficial is the way to go if you don't want to get hurt," Tara mused.

All this time, Katie thought, she had made it about her. And suddenly she could clearly see it was not about her at all. It was about a man who was trying desperately to show the world how fearless he was, when really the truth was he was afraid of the very same thing every other person on the face of the earth was afraid of.

He was afraid of getting hurt. Not physically. Anyone who had ever had a broken bone knew it could not hold a candle to a broken heart.

The topics moved on to other things. By the time lunch was done, wisely or not, Katie knew she and Tara were going to be the best of friends.

On Friday, knowing Dylan was gone to trek with camels in one more desperate effort to ward off the things that could really hurt him, Katie chose the flowers herself. She chose the flowers she had seen Dylan choose for his mother, the flowers he had chosen even when he didn't know they had meaning. She chose white chrysanthemums for truth, and she chose daisies for purity and loyal love.

Then she began to add her own touches, white heather for protection, and day lilies for motherhood. Finally she mixed in the last of her spring tulips, with their message of perfect love. She wove her heart into the bouquet for Dylan's mother, and she felt the sweetness of the flowers begin to weave healing into her.

She loved him.

And she loved him so intensely it did not matter if there was nothing in it for her. While he was in the Sahara she would let the love come out, once a week, in these bouquets for his mother.

The bouquet finished, she stood back from it. It radiated something so pure it took her breath away. It radiated love that gave instead of took, it had captured the essence of love at its best and purest. Katie closed her shop doors for the day and drove to Highlands.

An hour later she found Dylan's mother in her room. Dylan's mother was a handsome woman, her strong face dignified, her carriage regal. Her gray hair was coiffed perfectly, and she had on a lovely suit. But when she turned blue eyes exactly like Dylan's to her visitor, there was a sad blankness in them.

"Hello, Mrs. McKinnon." She saw Mrs. McKinnon looking at her anxiously, trying to figure out who she was, searching a memory filled with gaping spaces.

"You don't know me," Katie assured her gently. "I brought you some flowers."

His mother looked at the bouquet, smiled sweetly, touched each of the blossoms with trembling hands, seemed to forget Katie was there. The message of the flowers seemed to reach through her fog. For a moment, the blue of her eyes sharpened with clarity. She put her nose to them, and sighed with such contentment that Katie understood perfectly why Dylan had been so loyal about bringing them.

A care giver came in loaded with fresh towels. "Oh, the flowers!" she said. "Mrs. McKinnon's son usually brings them. And reads to her, shows her pictures from albums, brings videos of old home movies. I understand he's been away or is away right now, though."

The care giver admired the flowers and chatted while she replaced the towels about what a nice boy that Mr. McKinnon was, how loyal to his mother.

"She doesn't even know he's come, of course, poor dear," the aide said, and then left.

Katie looked around the room. There were remnants of the other bouquets he had sent. And other things. Poetry books, framed pictures, photo albums. There was a signed baseball, a TV over in the corner, with a video machine underneath it.

This was the side he'd always kept hidden. This was how much a man could love. So much that it could hurt him, drain him dry, take more than he had to give, especially if he was shouldering his burdens alone.

Katie picked up one of the poetry books, and went and sat on the edge of the bed, facing his mother's chair. She began to read.

Yellow sunlight, soft as a lover's kiss,
Touches the face, wrinkled now,
Of the one he loved in youth.
He does not see the age-glazed eyes,
Or the hair as silver as a frost-painted morn,
For he sees her through the lens of memory
Where she forever dances with whirling skirts
And flying hair
His heart remains unchanged
Denying a world that has faded.

Katie looked up from the book, and *felt* the love and courage and hope that had been poured into this room. She looked at Dylan's mother, and saw not the bewildered look of dementia, but instead the woman who had once been.

She saw the love this woman must have felt in her lifetime, the love that she had been at the heart of. It was love that had produced two wonderful children, a legacy that went on in that grandson that she probably didn't even recognize.

When Dylan's mother's soft hand crept tentatively into hers, Katie began to cry.

Dylan sat glumly in the airport terminal, baseball cap pulled low over his eyes so he wouldn't be recognized. His neck hurt from the tumble he'd taken off the climbing wall, and the thought of spending three weeks on a camel was about as appealing as having his toenails pulled out one at time.

It had always worked before! The relentless activity, the adrenaline rushes, had always been a balm and a distraction in the past.

But this time it wasn't working.

He was missing Katie so badly it hurt worse than his neck. How had she gotten such a hold on him? Why couldn't he just turn off the way he was feeling?

And then he knew.

Love wasn't a faucet that could be turned on and off at will. He loved her, and he could go wander around in the Sahara for the rest of his life, and it wasn't going to change that.

He'd been kidding himself about how *full* his life was. How *gratifying*.

An afternoon with Katie and a baby beat the hell out of jumping out of airplanes. Climbing rock walls.

It sure beat the hell out of riding camels.

His flight was called. He got up, took a few steps toward the life he no longer wanted and then stopped.

It was Friday. He didn't need to be going to the Sahara. He needed to go see his mother.

Suddenly, there under the harsh glare of the airport lights he got it: life's message wasn't that love changed so never risk it. The message was that everything changed, so grab the gifts you were offered when you were offered them; to treasure the time you were given with those gifts, because time was short. He realized he didn't want to waste a minute.

Dylan McKinnon had played baseball all his life. But suddenly he knew exactly what it meant to step up to the plate.

It meant to do the hard thing, even when you weren't ready, even when you didn't want to.

When he stepped out of the airport and raised his hand for a cab, he was stunned to discover that for the first time in a long, long time he felt like a free man. A man who was all done running.

Dylan paused in the doorway of his mother's room. He'd thought of stopping at a neighborhood grocery and picking up a bouquet, but somehow he wasn't going to be able to ever do flowers again without thinking of Katie.

Besides, he seemed to know a thing or two about flowers now. Not about their meanings, but about quality, how the petals should look on open flowers, how the buds should hold the promise of light inside of them.

When he saw the young woman sitting on the bed, his mother's hand in hers, her shoulders trembling with tears, he lurched to a halt.

Katie.

Seeing her filled him. The persistent ache that had been in him for two weeks quieted. That feeling of *needing* to do something stopped. Her shoulders were shaking. He realized she was crying.

Once upon a time, a woman crying would have sent him running the other way. Instead he walked in quietly, sank down on the bed beside her.

She looked up, startled, and for a moment there was something panicked in her face, and it stabbed him that he had caused her to feel like that. She looked as if she was going to get up and bolt, but he took her hand, kissed the top of it, drew her head onto his shoulder.

He saw the flowers. He had been buying flowers from Katie for a year. Her flowers were spectacular. And yet even he, self-acknowledged cretin that he was, knew this bouquet was different. It shone with a light from within.

And then he saw his mother was looking at him. A sudden smile lit her face, and he knew whatever light shone from those flowers, was shining from him, too. His mother, befuddled as she was, still recognized love, *unfaded,* as that poem he had read to her so many times had promised.

Katie pulled away from his shoulder, but not away from him.

"I thought you were riding camels in the Sahara," she said defensively.

"In the end I decided it sounded boring."

"God forbid you should ever be bored," she said, and then she did pull away from him.

"Are you angry at me?"

"That would imply I cared about you."

"Oh, Katie, my lady, we both know you care about me."

Her defenses crumpled and she started to cry again. He didn't feel the least bit impatient with her tears. He didn't feel annoyed. He didn't feel as if he needed to stop them.

"I wish you had told me," Katie finally said, "I wish you had felt you could trust me with this."

And it really said it all. His gift: never saying the things that needed to be said.

Hiding in quips and business and games, in adrenaline rushes and stupid new conquests.

"I haven't talked about it to anyone," he said. "It hurts too much."

"Sometimes things hurt less when you share them."

"It wasn't you I didn't trust, it was myself. What if I'm like my father? What if I can't be trusted to do the right thing when the going gets tough?"

"Hasn't the going gotten tough?" she whispered. She held up the book of poetry to him. "Haven't you done the right thing?"

"He doesn't come to see her, you know." It was as if he was making one last-ditch attempt to be right.

But Katie was never going to be the girl who saw him in the way he wanted to be seen. She was always going to be the girl who saw him as he really was.

Katie looked at his mother and then at him. "I think," she decided softly, "what she'd want more than anything else is for your father to be happy. That's what I'd want if—"

She stopped abruptly.

"If what?" he asked her.

She tossed her head and looked at him bravely. "That's what I'd want if it was you and me."

"He's abandoned her. She didn't deserve that. Oh, Katie, you should have seen her. It was always about everyone else. If there was one piece of cake left, she never had it. If there was money for a new sink in the bathroom or a bike for me I always got the bike."

"See? I'm right, then," Katie said firmly. "She's in that chair. The last thing she would want is for everyone to be trapped there with her. Love isn't a prison. Love wants people to be free."

He realized that's what love did. Real love. It set people free. It didn't take hostages, hold captives, demand great demonstrations, or gifts.

He remembered that sensation of freedom he'd felt at the airport when he chose the road that led back to her, to Katie, instead of the one that would have led him even further into the desert.

"And what if it was the one you loved in that chair?" he asked gruffly. If he'd inherited that gene from his mother, it could be him in this place someday. "Then what?"

"Are you worried it could be you?" she guessed softly.

The old Dylan would have scoffed at the word *worry*. But he nodded.

"If you're truly worried about ending up like this, maybe you should stop jumping out of airplanes. Off bridges." But then she smiled. "No, I'm kidding. I love that about you. That you live fully. That's what you teach me."

"And so, if I ended up like this?"

"Why then," she said, without hesitation, "I would bring flowers and read poetry. I would go through the photo albums, and I would show the old family movies. I would do exactly what you have done, Dylan."

"A captive?" he asked gruffly.

"A captive?" She looked askance at him. "Of course not. It wouldn't be a chore to me, or a duty. It would be an act of grace."

He looked at the flowers she had arranged, and felt the love brimming out of them. He looked at her face, and what he saw was a truth about himself being reflected back to him.

When he had started coming here to do things for his mother, it had been the first time in his life that he had really done something for anyone else with absolutely nothing in it for him. Most of the time his mother had not even known who he was. And yet still he had come, giving the gift of his time and his heart, doing things that did not come naturally to him, like reading her poetry, combing her hair. He had not recognized it for what it was.

But Katie was right.

It had been an act of grace, of the purest love.

And something more: a rite of passage. When a man was capable of doing something, finally, for another, with no thought for himself, with no thought for his own rewards, or his own comfort, then he was ready.

Ready to quit riding camels and throwing himself off bridges.

Ready to acknowledge his true heart and his true courage. He was ready to be trusted with houseplants and goldfish and maybe a puppy.

Most of all, he was ready to love Katie Pritchard.

His mother's hand was on his cheek, and when he looked in her eyes he saw recognition. Not of him, maybe. But of love, certainly.

"I usually take Mom down to the dining hall for supper," he said gruffly. "Do you want to come with us?"

"Of course," she said.

At the front door to the dining hall, he paid the three-dollar charge for visitors for his and Katie's meals. They sat down with heavy plastic plates. The entrée was shredded beef. It came with mashed potatoes and peas. Three delightful old ladies sang vigorous tunes, and his mother forgot her meal and clapped her hands.

Dylan sighed and met Katie's eye.

"Somehow," he said, "I'd pictured something a little different than this for our first official date."

"Is that what this is?" Katie asked, and she looked delighted.

He nodded.

"Really," she said, "what would be better than having dinner with a guy and his mother?"

And he knew she meant it. And he knew something else. He loved her beyond words.

CHAPTER NINE

DYLAN knocked on the front door of his childhood home. He had a pizza in one hand and a half sack of beer in the other. The flowerbeds had gone to seed. An old newspaper was caught in a dead shrub. Maybe some weekend soon, he'd come and clean them out. He knew it was the kind of thing Katie would like to do with him.

He liked the mental picture of them digging together in dirt. What he was learning about Katie, ever since that first "official" date six weeks ago, was that she loved the small everyday pleasures. Coffee at the outdoor café down the street from their businesses, holding hands in the park, watching the sun go down over the lake with a bottle of wine and a bag of potato chips.

But she was full of surprises, too. The first time he'd taken her on his motorbike she had wrapped her arms around him and screeched, "Faster. Go faster!" She had beat him to the top of the rock-climbing wall three times out of four, and looked down at him grinning fearlessly.

Oh, yeah, she was giving brand-new meaning to the word *fearless*.

And that was what brought him here.

He was ready to go to the next level with Katie, but

he had some of his own "stuff" that needed dealing with first. You could not come to a girl like Katie with blackness in your heart.

His dad opened the door, and Dylan saw that time did not stand still. His mother's illness had taken a toll on everyone. His father looked tired, his military bearing stooped, his hair thinner.

Dylan saw, not the man who had betrayed his mother, but the man who had thrown baseballs for him until it was so dark he could barely see the white of the ball coming out of the night. He saw the man who had hung a tire in a tree for him to practice pitching his fastball. He saw the man who had come to every single Little League game, the man who had cried like a child when Dylan had been signed to the Jays, the man who had told him it didn't matter, when his career had ended as suddenly as it had begun.

"I brought some supper," Dylan said.

His father looked so happy to see him, but wary, too. "I thought you were doing some damn fool thing with a camel," he said gruffly, holding open the door. "Damn shame to hear what your son's up to on the local news at five."

His dad was right. It was shame-on-him, that his father did not even know he had never gone on the camel trip. "Ah, I decided I could live life without adding the title of camel jockey to my résumé."

They ate pizza in front of the TV, watched sports, sipped cold beer. Dylan realized, his dad, just like him, and maybe all men, had trouble with emotion, with communication.

It would be so easy to not even speak of the rift that

had been between them, to just pretend it had never happened, to let the pizza and beer and his presence be apology enough.

But Dylan wasn't just here for himself. He was here to be a man big enough to acknowledge his own errors, big enough to forgive those others had made.

He was here to prove he was a man with enough heart and soul and ordinary garden variety guts to live up to the love of a woman like Katie Pritchard.

During a commercial, he took a deep breath, reached for the Mute on the remote control, and he cleared his throat. "Dad, I wanted to let you know I'm sorry. I know it was a hard enough decision for you, without me making it harder."

His father made a harrumphing noise that could have meant "Shut up" or "Go on," so Dylan charged on. "I know what Mom would want more than anything else is for you to be happy. For all of us to be happy. For the family to always be a family, even without her.

"I know we've lost her. I know she isn't ever going to be the way she was before, but, Dad, if we lose the lessons she gave us, that would be the real tragedy. She taught me what love means, and I feel really bad that I forgot that for a while."

His father put his head in his hands. "Okay," he said, and then he looked up, tears shining in his eyes. His tone was defensive. "She doesn't even know whether I go or not, Dylan."

"I know."

"It's not that I don't love her. You understand that, don't you?"

"Yeah."

"It's that I love her so much. It's not just that I don't want to see her like that, it's that I feel she wouldn't want me to see her like that. She put so much stock in this thing she called dignity. What would she think of me seeing her stripped of hers?

"We used to talk about what we'd do if one of us was on life support, with no hope. We both agreed that would be the gift we'd give the other one. We'd pull the plug. We both agreed that once the spirit was gone…" His voice faded. "It was supposed to be me, you know? That's how selfish I can be. I wanted to die first so I would never have to live without her. This is even worse, living without her, even though she lives."

They were silent, but the silence was without tension, two men contemplating the unpredictable twists and turns of life.

"Ah, maybe its time for you to go on that cruise, Dad."

"Maybe it is," his father said, and took the remote and turned the TV back up.

Dylan reached in his pocket and pulled out tickets. Two tickets. "For you and a friend," he said. "I'm going to be in Cabo San Lucas on these dates. Swimming with dolphins. I was kind of hoping you might like to meet me there."

When he left his father that night he went home and turned on his computer. Now he was worthy.

Now it was time to woo his woman. For real this time. Not part of a game, not with no clearly defined goal. Dylan knew exactly what he wanted. And he was pretty sure he knew how to get there.

He thought for a moment and then typed a phrase into the Internet search engine. He typed in *the secret meaning of flowers.*

Katie left work early, aware of feeling tense. What was going on with Dylan? For weeks now he had called her every day, wooed her, made her fall so far in love with him she couldn't believe such depths existed. She knew what it was to wake feeling as if you were walking on air, and to go to sleep with such a feeling of fullness, even if all you had to eat was potato chips and wine. Her life was more than she had ever dreamed it could be.

He'd called yesterday, but he'd seemed distracted, like a man with a great deal on his mind. He'd said something about visiting his father. She was aware of the estrangement, she had always known in her heart who he was, and that he would do the right thing. No matter what Tara thought, Dylan was no shirker when it came to the hard things.

So, instead of focusing on him, she had gone to see her own mom, and felt such a deep sense of appreciation for her, loved every minute with her. Her mother showed her the outfit she had bought to wear to the Tac Revol reading—a hideous black-and-white sweater suit embossed from head to hem with cats.

Katie had the horrible feeling she might have inherited her mother's fashion sense. But if she also had her joie de vivre, it was all good.

Now, the teeniest little doubt. Had he tired of her, returned to his old pattern? But here was the difference between loving Dylan and every other love she had ever experienced: if it ended it would leave her feeling richer and deeper and better than she had felt before, not depleted, not lacking, not as if there was something wrong with her. Loving Dylan had taught her life's most glorious secret: real love did not make a person feel afraid. No, it made them fearless, exhilarated, *exactly* what she felt when she reached the top of the climbing wall and looked down at Dylan.

She had seen herself through his eyes now. And she knew a delicious truth about herself. She was beautiful. She was deserving. She was worthy of this thing called love.

She unlocked her car door and went to slide in. She stopped, stepped back out and picked up a bouquet off the seat.

Dandelions! She glanced around. No one in sight. How had her door gotten unlocked?

Then she turned her attention back to her bright yellow bouquet, and allowed herself to feel the pure delight of the unexpected gift.

It was put together so carefully, so that it looked like a gigantic pom-pom, the stems tied with a ribbon, and wrapped with wet towel, then wrapped again in plastic.

Katie knew of only one man in the whole world with enough confidence, with enough of a sense of fun to leave a bouquet of dandelions!

And of course she knew, as few others would, in the old days, before there were flower shops, a man could pick his girl a bouquet of these anytime from spring to fall, reminding her that he would always be faithful, that her happiness meant everything to him.

Her eyes filled with tears. So, things had gone well with his father. Dylan was ready to embrace everything that love meant, including the hardest thing of all. Forgiveness.

Still mulling over her unexpected gift, she got home to find another. There on her small front porch stood a potted shrub. Dogwood, in full bloom. *Love undiminished.*

She gathered it up in her arms, and put it and the dandelions right in the middle of her kitchen table. And then she picked up Motley and, ignoring his shrill meows of protest, she waltzed him around her whole house. Should she call Dylan? Thank him?

No, it was his show. But even so, she could barely sleep that night. She was so restless the cats got up in protest and left her bedroom. She had a funny feeling the cats were going to have to get used to not sleeping with her soon, anyway.

She woke up Sunday morning to a knock on her door, but despite barely a wink of sleep she leaped from that bed like Cinderella going out the door to her awaiting carriage.

On her porch was an orange tree, heavy with blossom. The fragrance was absolutely heavenly, which went rather well with the traditional message of orange blossom.

Eternal love.

The tree was really much too heavy to lug in the house, but she could not bear to leave it outside. Her tiny house was soon filled with the scent of eternal love.

Nervous, she sat by the phone and chewed her fingernails, guarded her precious orange tree from the cats, who thought they should climb it. But as the day progressed, it occurred to her she had to do something productive with her time. She couldn't just wait around as if she was pathetic. She was more than that now! She was determined never to think of herself as pathetic again. That's what love did.

Katie went to her closet and threw out every single item of clothing that was not worthy of a woman totally, breathlessly in love. Then she lugged the orange tree into the bathroom and shut the door to protect it from the cats.

She went shopping and bought the wardrobe she had always wanted to have. It wasn't the sophisticated, glamorous wardrobe she had purchased for her life with Marcus. But it wasn't the wardrobe of a crazy cat lady, either.

It was the wardrobe of a woman filled to the brim with the confidence that being admired brought—flirty skirts and snug jeans, beaded blouses, sexy necklines, pajamas made of real silk.

She had just arrived home when the orchids were delivered. Like her other gifts there was no card, but then, she didn't need a card, because she had always known that flowers had a language of their own. Orchids spoke of love and beauty.

"How on earth did he get orchids delivered on a Sunday?" she asked the delivery boy.

"Hey, what would you do for tickets to a Jays game?" the boy said.

Again, despite a luxurious bath in her orange-blossom-scented bathroom, Katie had a sleepless night. She got up in the morning to find a sunflower on her porch. Bartholomew took an instant dislike to it, and she had to put it in the bathroom with her orange tree.

All the way to work she contemplated the meaning of sunflowers. They held in their sunny petals promises of devotion, reminders of sunshine even on days when the skies had turned gray.

That morning Katie had dressed more carefully than

she ever had in her life: a rich-chocolate embroidered skirt, tight, a matching jacket that dipped at her chest, hugged her curves. She dressed like a woman who knew she was beautiful, and worthy of all she was receiving. She dressed like a woman who tingled with the life force.

And then she arrived at work, opened her flower shop to find a single full-bloom rose, pink, on the counter. A single full-bloom always meant *I love you*.

Pink stood for perfect happiness. For all that this was wonderfully romantic, more than she ever could have dreamed for herself, Katie knew perfect happiness would be when he came forward, when he held her, when he took her lips with his own.

When they took up where they had left off that night at his sister's. But Dylan was surprising her by being the most patient of men, by wooing her with all the slow deliberation of those gents of Victorian times who knew the secret meaning of flowers and who knew a court-ship was as much about anticipation as it was about anything else.

The onslaught continued over the next few days: he sent red camellias, which meant she was a flame in his heart, and red roses that meant he loved passionately.

But, even though she dressed every day as if she would see him, dressed in a way that was guaranteed to make his eyes pop nearly out of his head, she saw not one hint of Dylan anywhere. When the white violet arrived, she decided she'd had enough. Her patience was at an end. She called his office, and was put through immediately.

But when she heard his voice, she felt suddenly shy, tongue-tied. "Okay," she finally blurted out, and repeated the message of the white violet. "Let's take a chance."

"How big a chance?" he answered back.

"You're the daredevil. You tell me."

"All right. I will."

Within ten minutes a box arrived. She opened it, and saw a departure from the flowers. Inside it was a hooded, sleeveless running jacket, with the Daredevils emblem on it. She put it on.

It looked absolutely dreadful, the bright red clashing with the soft bronze of her full skirt, and her high heels. Uncaring her look was now somewhat comic, Katie admired herself in the mirror, and felt more attractive than she had ever felt. After she was done admiring herself, she found a note inside the pocket:

"Pull the tab on the shoulder."

She did. A sleeve, light as silk, flowed down her arm like an accordion expanding. She laughed out loud, and pulled the tab at the other shoulder. Another sleeve, and this time another note:

"See Mrs. Abercrombie."

She went into her back workroom. She should have known he had a accomplice. Mrs. Abercrombie was not scheduled to work today.

"I thought you didn't like him," she said to her stalwart assistant.

"Well, I didn't. Not until I found out his intentions were honorable." Mrs. Abercrombie looked at her employer and smiled. "Finally," she said, "the rose blooms within you. Here, he said to give you this."

From underneath a curtained sink, she produced a plant. Smiling, she handed it to Katie, who began to tremble.

Ivy.

"I...I...I seem to have forgotten what ivy means," she said, but the truth was she had not forgotten at all, but was afraid to believe.

"Ah, well," Mrs. Abercrombie said, looking over her shoulder and slipping on her jacket, heading out the back door, "maybe it will come to you."

The door closed behind her, and she was shaking like a leaf. And then he cleared his throat, and she turned and looked at him.

How could he be even more beautiful than her memory had painted him? He was wearing a jacket identical to hers and was leaning against the doorjamb, a picture of male confidence. Except, maybe in the blue of his eyes was the tiniest bit of doubt, of concern.

"An ivy stands for wedded love," he told her. "For fidelity." Was his voice shaking ever so slightly, this daredevil, this man without fear?

"Yes," she said, amazed by her own sudden calm, "it does."

"The jacket looks great," he decided, changing the subject. "One of the nicer things I've seen you wear." He stopped, "Though I've got to say that skirt is phenomenal."

He'd noticed what she was wearing! He never noticed what she was wearing!

"It's a beautiful jacket," she agreed, "I love the sleeves."

"An old cyclist's trick. If you approve of the design, they're going into production next week."

"I love the jacket," she said again. What she meant was *I love the man who gave me the jacket.* "Could we get back to the ivy?"

"Oh, sure. You should look in the leaves," he said.

She found a small envelope. Inside was a necklace with

two diamond-encrusted dolphins jumping together. She was not sure she had ever seen a piece of jewelry so lovely.

"This is what I thought," he said. "You've already had the white-wedding thing. Do you want to do that again?"

She shook her head no. Somehow she had pictured a quiet beach and a setting sun, maybe some champagne and potato chips, bare feet in warm sand.

"This time I want it to be just for you. And me."

The tears were beginning to come and she could not stop them.

"I thought maybe we could go swim with the dolphins," he told her softly. "And, you know. Maybe get married at the same time. On the beach at a place called Land's End. Land's End. Love's beginning. After we get married, our families could join us for a holiday." He looked at her closely. "You aren't going to faint, are you, Katie, my lady?"

But he wasn't taking any chances. He came and scooped her up into his arms, twirled her around the whole flower shop, her dress whirling around them until they were laughing breathlessly.

"I've been wanting to do that ever since you took those stupid tickets for a dance instead of me," he confessed to her.

"Are you trembling?" she asked him.

"Yes."

"Are you afraid?"

"I was," he admitted, "before I heard your answer. I'm not afraid now. I think sometimes a person trembles when they are in the presence of something greater than they are. I am in the presence of love, and I have waited my whole life to stand here.

"I looked for it in so many places, places where I could not hope to find it, and I mistook so many imitations for this. But now that I have felt the real thing, I'm never going back, Katie." He whispered in her ear, "Like that poem my mother likes, you will never fade for me, Katie, my lady. My heart will remain unchanged. That is my vow to you."

In that moment Katie knew a truth about herself. She had come to doubt her instincts, but now she saw they had always been good. Her instincts—her heart—had spotted this man when he was just an anonymous guy in a track suit. No, her instincts were very good. It was when she did not listen to them that she got herself in all kinds of trouble.

Dylan McKinnon had shown her the way—fearlessly—back to herself.

Her instinct now was to kiss him.

And she did. She tasted the whole world in his lips, and part of heaven, too. She tasted the past that had led them to this place, and the future that was beckoning. She tasted the strength and joy that would bring them through hardship, the faith that would welcome their children to the world, the hope that all things could be healed.

And on his lips she caught the faintest taste of roses, and why not? For all time those flowers, more than any other, had brought the messages of men's hearts: desire, excitement, happiness, unity, passion, worthiness, gratitude.

Her soul opened like a rose, and her heart knew every secret a flower had ever told.

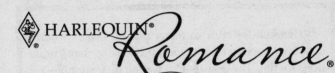

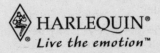

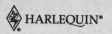

REQUEST YOUR FREE BOOKS!
2 FREE NOVELS PLUS 2
FREE GIFTS!

HARLEQUIN ROMANCE®

From the Heart, For the Heart

YES! Please send me 2 FREE Harlequin Romance® novels and my 2 FREE gifts. After receiving them, if I don't wish to receive any more books, I can return the shipping statement marked "cancel." If I don't cancel, I will receive 4 brand-new novels every month and be billed just $3.57 per book in the U.S., or $4.05 per book in Canada, plus 25¢ shipping and handling per book and applicable taxes, if any*. That's a savings of over 15% off the cover price! I understand that accepting the 2 free books and gifts places me under no obligation to buy anything. I can always return a shipment and cancel at any time. Even if I never buy another book from Harlequin, the two free books and gifts are mine to keep forever.
114 HDN EEV7 314 HDN EEWK

Name _____ (PLEASE PRINT)

Address _____ Apt. _____

City _____ State/Prov. _____ Zip/Postal Code _____

Signature (if under 18, a parent or guardian must sign)

Mail to the **Harlequin Reader Service®**:
IN U.S.A.: P.O. Box 1867, Buffalo, NY 14240-1867
IN CANADA: P.O. Box 609, Fort Erie, Ontario L2A 5X3

Not valid to current Harlequin Romance subscribers.

Want to try two free books from another line?
Call 1-800-873-8635 or visit www.morefreebooks.com.

* Terms and prices subject to change without notice. NY residents add applicable sales tax. Canadian residents will be charged applicable provincial taxes and GST. This offer is limited to one order per household. All orders subject to approval. Credit or debit balances in a customer's account(s) may be offset by any other outstanding balance owed by or to the customer. Please allow 4 to 6 weeks for delivery.

Your Privacy: Harlequin is committed to protecting your privacy. Our Privacy Policy is available online at www.eHarlequin.com or upon request from the Reader Service. From time to time we make our lists of customers available to reputable firms who may have a product or service of interest to you. If you would prefer we not share your name and address, please check here. ☐

HR07

HARLEQUIN
Super Romance

Bundles of Joy—
coming next month
to Superromance

**Experience the romance, excitement
and joy with 6 heartwarming titles.**

BABY, I'M YOURS #1476 by *Carrie Weaver*

ANOTHER MAN'S BABY
(The Tulanes of Tennessee)
#1477 by *Kay Stockham*

THE MARINE'S BABY (9 Months Later)
#1478 by *Rogenna Brewer*

BE MY BABIES (Twins)
#1479 by *Kathryn Shay*

THE DIAPER DIARIES (Suddenly a Parent)
#1480 by *Abby Gaines*

HAVING JUSTIN'S BABY (A Little Secret)
#1481 by *Pamela Bauer*

Exciting, Emotional and Unexpected!

*Look for these Superromance titles in March 2008.
Available wherever books are sold.*

HSR71476

HARLEQUIN *Romance*

Coming Next Month

**Join Harlequin Romance® in the fairy-tale mountains of Europe,
on the shimmering Italian coast, at a grand Australian estate—
and don't be late for an engagement in the boardroom!**

#4009 A ROYAL MARRIAGE OF CONVENIENCE Marion Lennox
By Royal Appointment
Life doesn't always turn out the way you plan, right? As heir to the throne,
Nikolai knows duty must always come first. But country vet Rose, his
convenient wife-to-be, is not quite what Nikolai was expecting....

#4010 THE ITALIAN TYCOON AND THE NANNY Rebecca Winters
Mediterranean Dads
In the first book of this emotional duet, nanny Julie is whisked away to
a palatial Italian villa, but feels completely out of place in Massimo's
glamorous world. Her biggest challenge, though, is ignoring her attraction
to the brooding tycoon....

#4011 PROMOTED: TO WIFE AND MOTHER Jessica Hart
Perdita's efficient, no-nonsense attitude works just fine in the boardroom.
But when she meets executive Ed, and their business relationship
becomes personal, she's left wondering whether being a wife and mother
would suit her better.

#4012 FALLING FOR THE REBEL HEIR Ally Blake
It's definitely true that opposites attract, and Kendall couldn't be more
different from Hudson Bennington III. She likes safe and secure—and he's
got danger written all over him! But then he proposes a deal, and Kendall's
tempted to accept....

#4013 TO LOVE AND TO CHERISH Jennie Adams
Heart to Heart
Sometimes we think we're better off coping with hardship alone, trying to
protect the ones we love. When Jack went away he broke Tiffany's heart,
but now that his demons are behind him, he's back—and determined to
make things right.

#4014 THE SOLDIER'S HOMECOMING Donna Alward
Shannyn's beautiful daughter is a daily reminder of her true love, Jonas,
who left town to be a soldier. Now that Jonas is back, hardened by war,
Shannyn must find a way to reach his soul again for the sake of her
daughter and the family she longs for.

HRCNM0208